RAY

SENECA
ELEMENT

THE SENECA SOCIETY BOOK II

Copyright © 2019 Rayya Deeb
All rights reserved.
RayyaDeeb.com

This book or any portion thereof
may not be reproduced or used in any manner whatsoever
without the express written permission of the author
except for the use of brief quotations in a book review.

Mediology Productions
12400 Wilshire Blvd., Suite 1275
Los Angeles, CA 90025

MediologyProductions.com

ISBN: 978-1-7342016-0-4

Library of Congress Control Number: 2019917459

First Print, First Edition 2019

Cover Design by Chris Thompson/Lucky Ember Design

amazon.co.uk®

A gift from **Rayya Deeb**

Enjoy your gift! From Rayya Deeb

Gift note included with **Seneca Rebel: The Seneca Society Book 1: Volume 1**

Explore Seneca

SenecaSociety.com

NO MIMES MEDIA
&
mediology

Acknowledgments

My biggest mistake in Seneca Rebel was not placing my acknowledgments in the front of the book. Many of you were right there with me from the beginning of the process, and even before that, so this is where you truly belong— front and center.

Aaron. I love navigating through all of this with you as my P.I.C. and the most dedicated father that two little girls could ask for. Thank you for constantly speaking with me about these fictional characters in Seneca like they are our friends. It's a pretty special thing that we can dive into a make-believe world together like it's totally normal. Well, it is *our* normal, and I love you for that, for the man you are, and for the woman you inspire me to be. I could not have written this book without you— this one even more than the last. I cherish our life together more than all the writerly words could ever express.

My mamma. This book wouldn't be if it wasn't for you. Thank you for guiding me to be me. Thank you for, once again, reading my pages with a red pen. Taking Simone to the library in the morning and then London again later in the eve. Often spending up to four hours a day at the Thousand Oaks Library with our little ones. Reading books, dropping knowledge and showering them with your love. You are a gift to me, to them and to anyone who has the good fortune of knowing you. I also credit you for accounting for at least half of Seneca Rebel's book sales. Thank you for that.

My two beautiful daughters— London and Simone. Being your Mamma is the greatest privilege life has given me. You inspire me beyond measure. Even when you drive me bonkers, you push me to grow. I am proud of you, I love you, I live for you, I write for you— hopefully to give back to you some of the inspiration and love that you've given me. Please don't ever stop being the kind, loving and curious individuals that you are, and don't ever be afraid to stand up for what you believe in. I love you, London.

I love you, Simone.

Marcus Lee. Magnus Kim. I thank each of you for caring and sharing your brilliant minds with me along this path: from notes on screenplays to legal contracts to marketing materials, to ice cream making advice and beyond.

Chris Tomasino. Thank you for being a tremendous voice of reason and pushing me to be smarter without even pushing.

Fallon Ureda. Thank you for sitting down with me and looking at these pages line-by-line and immersing yourself into the world and the work. You know part of this process was quite painful for me, but the part of it I experienced with you was the opposite. It's been a total blast imbibing your insight to make these pages glow. And Krista Howard. We clicked instantly with all sorts of laughs and long chats about my book and others too. Your opinions have influenced these pages and I thank you with my heart and soul.

Chris Thompson. Your passion for art shows in what you've done with this cover and so much of the design that accompanies the release of both books. Thank you for your enthusiasm and dedication.

Michael Shields. You are one of the most positive and persistent people I know. I appreciate the energy you invested in Seneca.

Pat Chapman. Thank you for the awesome Seneca Rebel teaser you cut for us.

My champions, confidants, collaborators and closest friends. You've done it again. Everyone I thanked in Seneca Rebel, I cannot thank you enough; for the success of the first book and for taking this journey with me through the second. I am filled with gratitude for every single person that invests their precious time into reading what I've written.

All of you unexpected, superstar supporters— cousins, friends of friends, my mom's friends. Wow. You have no idea the fuel you give me to keep writing. So many people have had my back; From old junior high, high school and college friends, to people I hadn't even met, like Douglas Grant. Thank you all for supporting me. Thank you for the reviews, the e-mails, texts, phone calls and social media posts. Thank you for reading Seneca Rebel (and now Seneca Element) from the airplane to the beach and sharing pictures… keep 'em coming!

London's and Simone's incredible teachers— Terri Arroyo, Mrs. Hanna, Pat Noe, Lisa Frangos, Karen Cyffka, Joshua Sarena, Casey Reimer, Mrs. Wood & Mrs. Martinelli and now Jen Barber and Karen Swanson. Kelly Lovenson, you are straight stardust. We hit the teacher jackpot! Thank you for sharing your kindness, strength, intelligence and love with our girls.

The moms I ride alongside, and my girls with whom I lunch, brunch and happy hour with, together and individually— you have enriched my life and I am incredibly grateful for your friendships.

Our neighbors on the legendary Avenue. You guys are too good to be true. It means everything that we have each other's backs the way that we do. Thank you for the bonfires, kickball games, crab fests, Halloween and everything in between. It really does take a village and ours is stellar.

Someone who dedicated her life to community, emphasis on unity— Judith Peters Beattie, or as I knew her, Mrs. Beattie. She may have passed away this year at ninety-five-years-young, but her spirit lives on in the hearts of so many. She will forever be in mine.

One Love

For my man.

1

SALT-LACED SWEAT seeped across my lips and hit the tip of my tongue. Pretty much running on empty, it was just the jolt I needed. My taste buds enjoyed the kick, so I licked a bit more, then sucked in a colossal breath, desperate to get enough oxygen at such a wicked elevation. I was born and raised at sea level, and this gargantuan wilderness somewhere between Cusco and Lake Titicaca, up near twelve thousand feet, was swallowing me. I was on my own with the moth-sized mosquitoes, monstrous spiders and smothering humidity and heat. Beads of perspiration trickled down my face, moistening the neck of my t-shirt. With blistered feet, breaths inconsistent and deep, I yearned for some of that thick, juicy oxygen I was used to back in Virginia.

Slammed up against the side of a mountain, I scaled along a muddy path, barely two feet wide. It was as if the entire scene had been plucked from a fantasy film and planted into the story of my life. To my left was a drop so immeasurable I couldn't bear to look down, but when I did, what I saw astounded and confused me: a neon-colored watermelon with purple, bloodshot eyes came to life. I watched as it tumbled down the mountainside in slow motion, smashing to smithereens on the rock candy-like ravine far below. That was exactly what could happen to my head if I wasn't careful.

Stepping backwards out of my own body, my right foot slipped on a patch of wet limestone, sending me careening over the edge. I grabbed for the ground, plastering both arms to the rain-slicked path, but when I felt my legs dangling over the cliff's edge, I knew I was doomed. My fingers dug desperately into the dirt but couldn't find a grip. The waterlogged skin of my fingertips tore off, and in the blink of an eye, I lost my hold on the earth. I plummeted, terrified. Ricocheting off rocks, I took a gash straight to the bone on my left arm. The cold air singed the tissue of the exposed muscle and I thought I was screaming my insides out, but there was no sound.

My body collapsed back against the wall of mud and exposed roots and I crumpled to the ground, grabbing at my arm. There were no gashes— my flesh felt fine. Better than fine. Marvelously smooth and sparkly, like diamonds. The sting of sweat trickling into my eyeballs combined with the potent Peruvian sun made me squint. I tried to blink thoughts away but my confusion only got worse. Black clouds rolled into my consciousness, bullying the innocent white ones off into someone else's dreams.

Seneca Element

The rain began as a sprinkle, and then the concussive sound of thunder hit. The storm rolled in quickly, shifting from oppressive heat to a wet cold. I undid the latch of the strap across my chest and yanked off the eggplant-colored canvas backpack. I pulled out the rubbery hooded raincoat that I'd picked up at the outfitters in Lima and put it on. With my arms squeezing the backpack tight, I curled into a ball right there on the side of the mountain and waited for the storm to pass. If this mountainside had been through so many storms before and was still standing, then I figured I'd be fine as long as I blended in with it, chameleon style. But then, as the dagger-like rain began to strike my body, the cold became unbearable. I grabbed the emergency blanket I had packed and wrapped myself in it, fearing I might freeze if the storm didn't end before nightfall. I shivered inside my soggy cocoon, teeth clanking uncontrollably, arms plastered to my body as I hugged myself, covered in goosebumps the size of pimples. All I could think about was getting to a lower elevation... if I could just survive the night.

The whole point of the trip was to get to The Seneca Society's Hub 48 entrance on Lake Titicaca and find my dad. I was determined to see if he was really there, and to finally discover the deeper, hidden secrets of this subterranean, technologically-advanced world. I had the coordinates for the covert entrance point, but somehow I'd become inexplicably disoriented. Now I was lost in the middle of nowhere, practically beaten to a pulp and starting to doubt my ability to find Hub 48 after all. And to make matters worse, I was disconnected from the data grid, without access to the superhighway of information and the network of people that could help me figure out the right way to go. All the planning I had done and the materials I had collected for this trip, now stored in my encrypted Veil, were completely inaccessible.

My Veil was my lifeline, everything— and I mean *everything* — important was there. It had the recognition data I'd borrowed from my friend, Brittany Gilroy, the daughter of a Seneca Senator, to get me into the Aboves in the first place, and keep me untraceable. It had all the maps I needed to find my way. It stored my passwords, health records, personal contact information... literally everything that meant anything to me. But now the harsh reality of making a successful trek while being completely off the grid was beginning to sink in. What if no one finds me out here?

My FlexOculi was going bananas. Up to this point I'd only had the experience of using it to project computerized images in front of my eyes on command. It was doing its own thing now, blasting disturbing imagery at me. It felt so real I couldn't tell whether or not it was. I was suddenly in this vortex of wet trees and vines that shapeshifted like flexers, all with minds of their own. Was my flexer implant letting me see an alternate dimension or was my mind playing tricks on me? It had been a hard decision to implant the flex into my body. The ways it enhanced and expanded my own human capabilities had proven many times over to be well worth the high risk that came with the invasive implant procedure. I thought this device inside me could be trusted even more than the people I loved, but now I was second guessing everything.

Which brought me back to thinking about my dad. Had he really chosen a life in Seneca over one with my mom and me? I had to believe that wasn't the case but I was desperate to find out. And Dom— man, did I love Dom. And now I'd lost him, too, without ever getting the chance to tell him how I felt.

Dom and I had been back together for two whole months after the debate— sort of the Bonnie and Clyde of the Seneca Education and Research Center, or as we called it, S.E.R.C. I was addicted to the butterflies and he was addicted to my butt— always grabbing it. Let me be clear: if anyone else, ever, in my entire life, had grabbed my butt, I seriously would have roundhouse kicked them. But, with Dom, it was different. It let me see a playful side to a guy that was always so intense. I felt accomplished in some strange way, to have brought out that side of him. But it was serious business when he kissed me. Like he had this whole world to give. I never knew a kiss could have that power.

I craved his kiss again as I lay on the mountainside. The sting of salt on my lips reminded me of the last time I had been moved by Dom's touch, before everything had come crashing down.

2

FROM THE FIRST moment I saw Blue Combat Boots, I was consumed beyond reason, which was completely out of character for me. Dominic Ambrosia. His essence is so powerful that it stays with me, even when we're apart. It's weird how I can wish I'd never met him, but at the same time want to be with him like crazy. The hours spent together had always vanished as if no time had passed, and in those moments I'd let myself go. I'd become hooked.

During Operation Crystal, I was engulfed in this fully-fledged Dom-fog. The job of deactivating illegal nanobots appearing in the blood of Senecans had been assigned to Dom and me by Seneca's governing body, the Seneca Senate. Our discovery of this scheme by underhanded Senecans was a huge coup, but it also ended up being incredibly dangerous for us. Some of the individuals who'd spearheaded the use of the nanobots had been members of Seneca Observation and Intelligence League—S.O.I.L., the internal Seneca organization that was still in charge of security there. They had decided that Dom and I were a threat to their systems and attempted to have us exiled to the Aboves. Ultimately, after a huge fight to stay in Seneca, we came under the protection of the Seneca Senate, and that's when they put us to work in Operation Crystal, eliminating the nanobots. I should have been completely focused on the task at hand, but I was mesmerized by Dom and that totally affected my thinking.

Here and now, in South America, I tried my darndest to shove Dom out of my thoughts so I could use my flagging energy to navigate out of the wilderness. Thoughts of him kept haunting me, though. Curled up inside my soaked gear, I even believed I heard his voice echo through the thunder, "Doro!" It jostled me — it sounded perfectly authentic. Could he really be here?

"I love you, Doro!"

I peeked out of my hood but I couldn't see him. Was I delirious? It wouldn't be the first time on this trek I thought I'd seen or heard something that wasn't real.

"Dom?"

"I'm staying right here with you, no matter what."

Whoever was messing with me, it had to end. "Stop!" I screamed. "Please, just stop!"

"Don't shut me out, Doro, I need to help get you through this —"

But I *was* shutting down. I felt a disconnect between my mind and body. I couldn't push the words out of my mouth because I couldn't even find the right ones. My eyes burned and I could barely lift my heavy head.

"I don't understand what's happening!"

"We can try and make sense of everything that happened between us later. Right now we need to get you to safety!"

"Dom?!"

"Doro, I need you to follow my directions, okay?"

I nodded my head.

"There's a cave ahead. I am going to guide you there."

"I can't!" I shook my head hard.

"You can!"

"No! I'm frozen!" My teeth chattered uncontrollably as I yelled gibberish out into the storm.

"I know, I know. God, I wish so badly that I could warm you up right now. I'm sorry, Doro, I'm so sorry."

My consciousness began to fade. Dom's presence waned as I slipped out of my body one moment and then back in the next, wedged between what felt like my reality and some other realm I couldn't recognize or define.

"If you don't get out of this freezing rain, you'll die!" Dom's cries rippled with panic. Was his voice just a figment of my imagination? As hard as I could, I tried to force my eyelids to part. A splattering of rain and dirt smacked me in the face. I wiped the gritty mess away with the back of my cold, wet, rubbery sleeve. A sudden drive to survive at any cost surged through me.

A six-inch, hologram FigureFlex version of Dom, was suddenly projected in front of me. He was one thousand percent focused on me. His presence was so lucid that for a wrinkle in time I forgot where I was. I was with Dom and he was with me and nothing else mattered. I tried to speak but the sound I emitted was garbled.

"Doro, please try to hear what I'm saying—"

Dom's unwavering gaze, his crunched, tight brow and the gravity in his voice scared the hell out of me, as if he knew of an imminent danger beyond my scope.

I became paralyzed in fear. I couldn't speak. I retreated back inside my cocoon. I had to regroup to figure out what was happening. Was my flexer even real? Was I living in some twisted simulation of my life? I just wanted this flex turmoil to end! I wanted to be back with my mom and Killer curled up in a ball in my bed.

"Come on, Doro, come back to me—"

I ended the FigureFlex.

Suddenly alone, I shuddered as the unrelenting rain pelted down on me. My mind couldn't sustain its present torment, so it took me back to a time when my heart had been the part of me doing all the suffering. I flashed to the Monday night in S.E.R.C., before I'd set off for the South American Seneca hub to look for my dad. I found myself in a scene that I couldn't stop reliving— the last time Dom and I had seen each other.

I waited next to the door to "our closet" in S.E.R.C. at our appointed meeting time, but Dom hadn't come. My FlexOculi monitor was up, and I was wondering when I'd get a flex from him explaining why he was late. I tried to flex him three times, but he didn't reply. Considering the amount of planning we'd done leading up to this crucial juncture, I couldn't comprehend why, when 7:05 p.m. hit, Dom still hadn't shown up. Recalling our unpleasant history with the inglorious S.O.I.L., I'd started to freak. What if they knew about our plans? As The Seneca Society's top intelligence agency, they knew practically everything about everyone. And by now Dom and I knew for sure that certain individuals inside that organization would go to any length to control all of the information inside Seneca. This time, though, we'd thought that we had out-foxed them once again, like we had with the nanobots.

But what if Brittany Gilroy had sold me out? She was the daughter of a Seneca Senator and I'd thought I could trust her— and that she trusted me, too. When would I learn to pay attention to the cynical lesson to 'trust no one but yourself'? When you deny what experience teaches you over and over again, you're going to find yourself completely screwed. I was afraid we'd stepped right into it.

"Campbella."

"Reba!"

It was an incredible relief to see him, but he had a look about him that unsettled me. Reba's special strength was his intuition, an intuition that was stronger than that of all the grandmas in the world, combined. I'd vibed with his spirit from the very first moment I'd set foot inside S.E.R.C. last year and we'd become great friends.

"It's 7:08," Reba said.

"Dom hasn't shown," I said, hoping he had answers.

"I was worried about that."

"Why?"

"Listen, chica, sometimes people fall out of sync... they get caught up in other things in life... but you can't let that stop you."

What was he talking about? I could tell Reba had information he thought would hurt me but was important enough for me to know. He just didn't know how to tell me.

"Reba, where's Dom?"

"You're wasting your energy getting hung up on Dom. The important thing to remember is that the truth is out there for those who seek it. You shouldn't be worried about anything else but that right now. Finding the truth. *Your* truth."

"Okay," I said as he avoided meeting my eyes. "I'm going to Colombia to find my dad no matter what, but I can tell you're keeping something from me, and I need all the intel I can get right now."

"You're right."

This was no time to play games.

"So?"

Reba's voice lowered, partly to keep the conversation just between us, but I think, too, because he wanted to soften the blow of what he had to say. "Listen, you shouldn't go to Colombia. You need to find your way in through Hub 48, in Peru."

I gave him a 'what-in-the-world?' look.

"I just feel that you should be headed to Peru rather than Colombia... I think that's where your dad is. I can't let you go off in the wrong direction," he said.

I had more faith in Reba's insight than my own. Which was crazy because I'm normally such a hard-evidence kind of girl. Science, facts, math— you know. They're my normal, reliable guides. While I believed in Reba's instinct, my own practical nature was kicking in.

"If your dad is as good a mathematician as you are—"

"He's the best."

"Then he would be working on the top secret projects going on in Peru. Seneca records show that Peru is where high up scientists live in order to protect them and the sensitive knowledge they have, to keep it from getting into the wrong hands."

"I see."

It added up. My father had been working on secret science

stuff before he'd disappeared. Reba's news was exactly the information I needed to help me find him. I was going to Peru.

"That and... one other thing. Dom knows, Doro..."

"Dom knows what?"

"He knows that he was framed for the flighter crash. He knows that you knew and never told him."

My heart jolted. Oh no.

"It's not your fault. You were trying to protect him, but the rumors were swirling and it was only a matter of time before it all came out."

My head sunk. I realized why he hadn't been flexing me back and it made perfect sense.

"So he's not coming with me?"

"I'm afraid not."

3

WITH A SLIGHT headache and a lump in my parched throat, I took a seat on the acoustic carrier. It was unusually quiet considering it was fueled by sound waves rather than electricity or gas. The stuff with Dom weighed heavy on my mind, but I managed to find solace in the silence of the ride. I loved traveling via this train-like transportation vessel. It was nice that the other passengers were chill as well, seemingly respecting the tranquility.

I knew Dom would be at Ty's Sushi, Reba didn't have to tell me, and so Ty's was a pit stop I had to make before I set off on my journey. I could just picture Dom like someone in an old time movie hunched over a bar wallowing in their sorrows, he just did it at a sushi bar created by his best friend.

On my ride to Seneca City's restaurant district I projected my FlexOculi screen and tuned in to a stream from Seneca's own news network, B3 News. It played a few inches in front of my face, and of course nobody else on the acoustic carrier could see what I was watching. The Incognito Mode setting had become a super fun way to consume media.

A newscaster's booming voice-over warned, *"World Health Organizations in the Aboves have announced that ultraviolet radiation in many locations has reached levels too potent for people to be exposed to. Until yesterday, there was a thirty minute daily safe exposure limit for direct exposure, but scientists now recommend no one goes outside, unprotected, for any length of time. It is strongly advised that UV suits and protective goggles should be worn outdoors to avoid damage to DNA at a molecular level. It is too early to determine all of the dangers but the immediate effects are alarming. World Health Organizations are reporting levels of cataracts and snow blindness increasing at alarming rates in unprotected animals..."*

While video images moved in and out across my monitor, a live, 3D satellite image of bright yellow UV pockets spreading across a black representation of the Earth came into view. Then there was a news feed from the Aboves of an extremely bright outdoor area at a shopping center with people walking around in metallic colored suits and clear, full-head helmets.

The newscaster continued with urgency, *"Global authorities have been tirelessly researching ways in which to create massive UV shields, but nothing has been presented to the public."*

Video images showed a mining operation. A clear cylinder the circumference of the Eiffel Tower shot up through the center of a dome and into the sky. An entourage of people in both power suits and white body suits worked inside the clear domed-in digging site at a lake.

"Researchers are tirelessly at work on a solution, but the reality that we now face is that without the layer of ozone in the stratosphere, life as we know it will very soon be over."

Someone in that entourage suddenly caught my attention. I rewound and paused as I spotted a face I knew intimately: the one and only Ellen Malone. What was she doing there? And more importantly, what were they all doing there? My eyes narrowed on the logo emblazoned on the machinery in the background. The logo read 'S.G.E. Corp.', the same company that Ellen had told me used to operate a power station at Claytor Lake. The company was run by Senator Wallingsford's brother, Billy. S.G.E. Corp and Ellen, had something to do with this operation. But what exactly?

I was mesmerized by Ellen from the moment we first met when she came to my Culver City apartment to recruit me to The Seneca Society. The offer came somewhat as an ultimatum though. She would be providing me a safe-haven from the fall-out of getting busted running an offshore gambling hack enterprise. If I hadn't accepted her offer, my mom would have taken the fall for my wrongdoings, and that meant jail time. Of course I took Ellen up on her offer.

As we reached the stop and I hopped off the acoustic carrier, I powered down my monitor. All I could think about was that all Senecans had loved ones in the Aboves they had to worry about on an entirely new level. They could hear news about them and think about them, but they couldn't communicate with them. This was par for the course with the agreement people made when they accepted Senecan citizenship and relinquished whatever citizenship and contacts they had in the Aboves. Things weren't looking good for human existence and that wasn't just some wild, apocalyptic theory. It was the new reality we were all facing. I knew that hyper-technologically-advanced Seneca was a means to Earth's solutions, if there were any, but not if it was stifled by some insane, corrupt power struggle that would only provide resources to well-connected people.

I stood at the back of Ty's Sushi, the ever-bustling eatery where Dom had a secret lab in the back until he and I got busted uncovering the nanobots in our bloodstreams. Dom sat by himself at the sushi bar with random people on either side of him. There wasn't an empty seat in the house so I approached him from behind. I hesitated for a moment before saying his name.

"Dom."

He didn't answer. I felt a dagger twist into my stomach because based on his pause, I knew he was pissed and about to ream me out. My sweet fluttery butterflies were miserable and sick.

"What are you doing here?" he asked. His words felt ice cold. He didn't even turn around.

I wished we could flash back to the first time we were here together and start all over, knowing what we needed to know now minus all the icky stuff. "Will you look at me?" I asked.

Dom stood up and turned around. His sunken eyes crawled up to mine.

"What's going on?" I asked, even though I already knew.

I realized I'd probably made him cry and that made my stomach cringe. I literally couldn't stand up straight.

"How can I look at you?" he asked.

His words crushed my heart.

"Dom, I am so sorry."

"Does that make *you* feel better? Apologizing?"

"Nothing makes me feel better about this."

Dom pulled his lips tight together and narrowed his eyes, looking into mine. Oh man, if looks could kill.

"I was so wrong, Doro. I was so, so wrong. I actually thought we trusted each other and that's what hurts the most."

"We do! I didn't lie to you, Dom."

"You did, though, and it's just completely messed up, Doro. That was information that I should have known and you know that!"

"But I didn't know—"

"Really? You didn't think I should know I was being framed for that crash? Wouldn't you want to know if it was you?"

"Who told you that?"

"*That's* your response? I can't believe you, Doro. Think about what I shared with you when we first met. And now that we know each other on a much deeper level *this* is how you treat me?"

Ty walked up to say hello, then noticed the tone of our conversation and quickly scurried away.

"You're right, Dom, but I just didn't know what to do. At first I was protecting you. Then you were so into our gig on Operation Crystal, I didn't want to mess anything up. And then more and more time passed and it was like I should have told you earlier, but I didn't, and I felt like you'd be so upset when I finally did."

"I *am* upset," Dom said.

"And I *am* sorry." He had to forgive me. What we had was too good to be ruined from one mistake on my part. I wanted to hug Dom so bad, but I could tell by his closed-off body language that he wanted none of that. So I searched for the right thing to say. "I swear I wasn't trying to hurt you, and I swear nothing like that will ever happen again."

"Right. Okay."

It seemed nothing I could say or do would change Dom's mind. I was backed into a corner and there was only one way to go from here. I was about to have to go to South America on my own and that was my own doing.

"Okay. Never-mind. Enjoy your sushi."

"Don't flip this on me."

"I messed up, Dom, but now this *is* on you! *You* didn't show up and you know how important this is to me!"

"It's not all about you, Doro!"

It suddenly got quiet around us and I felt people starting to stare, but I just looked square into Dom's eyes and at nobody else. He clamped his lips down even tighter, cutting me with his sharp gaze. People started to talk around us again, but I didn't want to risk being heard at all, so I leaned in and spoke in a hushed voice.

"Something insanely sketchy is going down in Seneca and you know it. You're the one who brought this all up to begin with. I mean, why else would they want those bots in everyone? You know this is huge and now we're in too deep to turn our backs! *Everyone* is in danger. I know this isn't about *me*!"

I couldn't stand to see Dom's face looking at me like I was awful anymore. I turned to go and didn't hesitate.

"Doro, wait."

I wasn't going to let him, or anyone, hold me back. I didn't stop, and as I approached the front of the restaurant I heard Dom call out, "Good luck!"

I paused in my tracks. It was like I'd been shot in the back by someone that I loved. That was the worst "Good luck!" in the history of my universe and Dom knew very well that I did *not* believe in luck. It was a dual-pronged dig and I couldn't believe that was how it was going to be between us. Just like that my heart was blown to pieces. Rather than try and pick it all up and put it back together, I left my heart there splattered across the cold, hard floor.

4

A TREMENDOUS WEIGHT tugged at my heart. It felt like suction cups were pulling me downwards, from the front of my shoulders, through my chest. I felt unreasonably cloudy. This untamable feeling stuck with me as I trudged through the mud the morning after the storm.

Slivers of sun began to slice through the towering Ceiba trees, slowly drying the moisture from my skin. I reached my hand up to the rays. Suddenly, out of thin air, FlexCore signaled me. I stopped dead in my tracks. I was back on the grid! Relief swept in like a breath of fresh air. I scanned my FlexOculi, studying all of my incoming nutrition data. My implant was communicating my health vitals with FlexCore, providing real-time computerized calculations on my caloric needs: vitamins, fats, proteins, etc.

My FlexCore's recommendations were on point. I knew exactly what I needed to eat, and when I needed to eat it for optimal body performance. In that moment, it was suggesting that I consume a source of iron and vitamin B12 as soon as possible. Although information hadn't been coming in consistently, or at all for the past day at least, FlexCore had recorded all of my nutritional activity and scanned every potentially edible object I passed for two days— *two days*?! I couldn't confirm or deny that because I couldn't differentiate between one hour and twenty-four. And how much of that time would I have been awake? Had I blacked out at all? Calories. The FlexCore data was right, I needed calories and water.

I winced as I stepped on something sharp— "Oww!" I looked down to see that I was somehow barefoot. Somewhere, it seemed, I had lost my hiking boots. My feet were caked in dirt and who knows what else. The grime was so thick I couldn't even see my toenails. The bizarre sounds of the mountainous terrain hadn't ceased since I had stepped into it. The natural surround sound was even more hardcore than the Virginia outdoors. My eyes darted in every direction, searching out any movement, any sign of life, and hoping for a friend yet dreading a foe.

Like a bolt of lightning there came my sign, in the form of an incoming FigureFlex. The possibility of human connection, albeit virtual, cranked me up.

"Reba!"

I slammed my finger onto *'Accept'* and there he was, a static 3-D projection of Reba, glitching off and on with the poor connection. "Campbella!"

Overjoyed to see him and convinced I was going out of my mind, I started to cry. Reba reached out for my shoulder, but I couldn't feel him and he couldn't feel me. I was with him, but I wasn't.

"Don't worry. We have a plan to get you out of there, but we need your help," Reba said.

Who was *we*? Ellen? Dom? Gregory Zaffron, that wretched S.O.I.L. agent that had fought to have Dom and me banished from Seneca altogether? I tried to force those thoughts to stop. Reba wasn't against me. He was gentle and authentic and one of my best friends. Why would he be cooperating with Gregory Zaffron? I had a glimpse of just how irrational that thought was, like it wasn't even mine to begin with. Or maybe Reba *was* against me. I couldn't stop those suspicious trains of thought. I started to retrace every moment Reba and I had shared. Had he known about the Necrolla Carne vaccine that was required of every new Seneca citizen, and that it was actually a nanobot virus S.O.I.L. had put in all of us? Was he aware of the programmed mosquitoes S.O.I.L. sent to attack me in the woods when Dom and I were on the run after I had reinstated his memories that S.O.I.L. had wiped… did Reba know all of it?

"Dom is here. He wants to flex you," he said.

My knees buckled me to a seat in the mud. I was as grungy as Seattle in the nineties and I really didn't care but I couldn't let him see me like this.

"Not right now," I replied.

Reba was taken aback and I could see why. He'd witnessed me go schoolgirl for Dom since day one and now I was telling him I'd rather Dom not flex me. But I was on my own and my mind was consumed with the search for answers.

"Campbella?"

"I just don't get it..." I said, "You appear out of nowhere, but I have no idea what you want or who you're with."

"I don't want anything, I'm trying to help you. Come on, you know I've always had your back."

"I'm not sure of anything right now. One guy is always keeping secrets, and the other wouldn't accept my apology, so now I'm on my way to a foreign Seneca hub, on my own."

Reba looked worried, but remained level-headed. "I told you Colombia was the wrong direction. Remember, Campbella? I know you do—"

"And look at me now. *This* was the right direction?"

"Exactly what Anika said *could* happen with your flex implant *is* happening, Doro. It's why we searched so hard to find you. You've been hacked."

Huh?

That, I did not expect.

Shock. Confusion. Denial. They hit me all at once.

But maybe...

No.

"Oh come on, Reba. Don't you think I would know if I'd been hacked?"

"No. You wouldn't. That's not how it works. Actually, part of it enhances your paranoia by sending interrupters into your critical thinking to trigger a fight or flight response, so you will most likely *think* what I am telling you is a lie. You really have to try hard to silence all the noise in your head and listen to your heart."

I couldn't believe it. I felt totally normal, and my feelings were all I could trust because they were real. They couldn't be faked. They were inside me like helium and that helium was vigorously pumping. I floated up into the air rising above all of this low-lying confusion where I could see everything for what it really was. It was clear that Dom hated me, so I couldn't possibly imagine why he'd be trying to help. There had to be something more to his actions. I was certain someone had put him up to it.

And then Dom flexed me.

I zoned in on 'Accept' and 'Decline.' 'Accept.' 'Decline.'

'Decline.' 'Decline.' 'Decline.' 'Accept.' Back and forth rapidly, my weary, fidgety eyes leapt. I told myself, *hit 'Decline.'* Stop the madness, keep moving forward, stay on the mission. This kind of uncertainty had already wounded me before.

I hit 'Accept.'

There he was.

There. He. Was.

"Doro."

Face to face with hologram Dom. He looked better than ever and I wanted so badly to hug him. I wanted to lay my head in the nook above his shoulder, get that subtle wisp of musk and cedar, the faint sensation of his heartbeat with my cheek against his neck, and forget all about the ickiness of the recent days leading up to the present. His hair had grown in and it was kind of curly and dirty blond, unexpected because I always thought of him as a straight-haired brunette, but this worked. It *really* worked. Seeing Dom there in Peru opened the floodgates to my heart. I didn't even know where to begin, what to say to him. My emotions yanked me from one direction to the next: love, anger, sadness, desire, confusion and an overwhelming feeling of uneasiness for not being forthcoming with the truth. I was paralyzed by the emotional tug of war going on inside and I couldn't say a word.

Dom and Reba. These were the two best guys in my life. But then I imagined them conspiring together just moments before this. Figuring out how they were going to stop me on behalf of S.O.I.L. Because if Reba is so intuitive (as the Intuerians are supposed to be the masters of this domain,) wouldn't he have told me not to get the Necrolla Carne vaccine to begin with?

Wouldn't he have said we shouldn't go to the party where the son of notorious Seneca Senator Frank Wallingsford, G.W. Wallingsford, crashed the flighter? Had he the inclination that Dom would have been framed for it and then banished to the Aboves with a wiped memory? Maybe Reba wanted Dom to be banished.

Whose side was Reba really on? Had he manipulated Dom in his vulnerable state of being upset with me?

My stomach turned in unison with every one of those thoughts that crossed my mind. They had to have teamed up, because otherwise none of this made sense. Ellen, Reba, Dom. They were all suspect. The entire lot of them.

Dom looked at my grubby, bare feet.

"I shouldn't have ever let you go alone," he said quietly as he looked into my eyes. We were so right together. Our souls connected in such a supernatural way and I didn't want it to disappear again, but I was torn in half. There were too many "What-ifs?" firing off in my mind, casting waves of doubt upon Dom and Reba, and I couldn't stop them.

I couldn't let myself respond to my heart believing that Dom's overture of care and compassion was completely genuine. The suspicions were too strong and oozing with logic. My logical brain was screaming at me as my heart melted into his. Tears streamed down my face. I wiped them away and closed my eyes, trying to stop my mind from thinking for just a moment.

"You're in trouble, Doro. *We're all* in trouble, and I want to help more than I've ever wanted to do anything."

What felt like a rational thought suddenly occurred to me—"Is Ellen Malone with you guys?"

Dom looked at me like I was speaking an alien language. "What? No."

Reba interjected, "Campbella, it's just us. Your boyfriend and your best bud. You have to know we are one hundred percent on your side."

I didn't know that. I didn't blame them for me coming on my own. I understood why Dom was mad and Reba was never supposed to come. But now I was in this position, and maybe it was exactly the position they wanted me to be in. I'd better play my cards right by not listening to them at all and letting them crash into my head. I needed every ounce of consciousness I could get. If Dom and Reba really cared, what took them so long to reach out to me? Why now? The only reason could be that they were up to something unspoken, something they were keeping from me. I had to get away from them. I was too weak. But at the same time, I wanted them. I was beyond happy to see them. I was elated. My whole body buzzed in their presence.

"Doro, we need to stick together right now. I know you can understand the reasoning that your mind has been compromised and the people who care about you want to fix that."

Me? Shutting *him* out? Was this even real? Was this some

computer-generated version of Dom? Because we were both speaking to different realities. Suddenly hologram Ellen glitched in. She was wearing the very same suit she wore when she came to recruit me.

I gasped. I blinked. As quickly as she appeared, she was gone.

"Ellen," I mumbled. The words started getting harder to push out of my dry, cottony mouth.

Reba desperately wanted to reassure me. "You really need some clean water."

His desperation almost tripped me up, but then I felt that that was his intention: to play to my heart and trick my mind. Didn't they realize I was onto them? Ellen was just standing right there! As I was running this over in my mind the graphic watermelon with purple eyes that tumbled down the mountain glitched in. It rolled behind a massive tree stump just to my left and I dragged my increasingly unresponsive body over to look for it. The flickering holograms of Reba and Dom floated along with me as I moved.

"What are you seeing, Doro?" Dom asked.

I couldn't answer, I didn't know.

Reba grew more and more worried by the second. I could tell by the way his voice shook as he said, "Doro, you lost connection to the grid because your flexer implant has been hacked."

"By who?"

"That's the thing. We don't know yet."

"Come on."

Dom chimed in, "Doro, it's the truth."

"And because you are saying it I should automatically believe it?"

Reba was taken aback. I kind of was too, but I wasn't at the same time. I felt way off.

"You know I'd never lie to you," Dom replied, quietly.

"*No*, I don't!" I could tell that burned him by the way he flinched at those three words, but we weren't exactly in happy-go-lucky-couple mode at the moment, prancing through fields of daffodils into the sunset. I knew quite well that my not telling Dom about the flighter crash was wrong but what these two were doing to me was way worse than that. I wasn't just going to sit back, blissed out and ignorant, with butterflies, because Dom popped up in hologram and said he cares.

At the same time, Dom apparently wasn't going to give up trying. "Well, whether you believe me or not right now, I *am* going to tell you this because I know you, Doro, and I know that eventually you will. There is an anonymous faction in Seneca with eyes and ears everywhere, from the C.I.A. in the Aboves to S.O.I.L. We're pretty sure it's them doing this to you."

"Is this leading up to you guys blaming Ellen? Because she's the easy target?" I asked, knowing full well they would feed me the answers they wanted me to hear regardless of the truth.

Reba proclaimed, "Ellen is the one who hinted us toward the Colombia hub to begin with, and Anika helped us get here! We've been trying to get to you for weeks!"

"Well maybe you shouldn't have."

What was I doing? My heart questioned everything my head forced me to say. My insides were out of sync and that twisted my guts up into a massive knot.

Ellen abruptly flickered in again, this time between Reba and Dom!

I looked at my FlexOculi and slammed my hand downwards onto 'Disconnect' for Dom, and then Reba stuck his hand out. "Don't!"

Poof— Reba vanished.

The guys were both gone. Gone, baby, gone.

Hologram Ellen smiled.

I ran.

And ran, and ran, and ran. The thick, cold mud splattered all the way up my tired legs. My pants were wet and heavy from the rain and that slowed me down.

I lost my breath. An intense cramp materialized in my right calf muscle. I bent over to rub it, trembling in pain. I was so dizzy the sky became the ground. Clouds bounced off the earth. I spotted a clearing inside a grouping of weathered trees. No one would be able to find me if I posted up for a breather in there. But then, right in front of me, there appeared a snake! A giant, fast-moving, bright green snake and it saw me. It was coming right for me! I turned to run.

5

I STIRRED AWAKE to a low, raspy voice with a Latin accent. "I'm still here."

Oh boy. *Still?*

I realized I had goggles on and tore them off because I had no memory of putting them on.

"You need to keep those on, or you will damage your eyes."

I rubbed at my eyes with the back of my clammy hand and pulled the goggles back over my eyes. I saw a guy's blurry figure about two feet away. This habit of waking up with strangers kneeling before me was something I needed to kick. The last one was Anika, and I trusted her. But I most definitely wasn't trusting this guy with... dreadlocks and a Jimmy Cliff t-shirt? Hmm, I do like Jimmy Cliff, though. I quickly began to adjust to the fact that he could kill me and sell my organs, and quite honestly, at that point, I really didn't care. Maybe, just maybe, he wouldn't kill me, I reasoned to myself, because from the looks of me right now, my organs weren't worth squat. In Seneca they were growing them like weeds.

"You had nightmares all night," he said, very matter-of-factly.

I was floored— all night?! With this guy?! How could I be so unaware of my surroundings? Had someone drugged me? What was happening to me? What happened last night? How many nights had I forgotten? Severe knots began forming in my gut, a direct response to the warning signals fired off by my mushy brain. I started to get choked up, but then I remembered I was not alone.

"Have some water," he offered, and I suddenly had déjà vu. It triggered the events of the past few days to come rushing back to me.

I recalled the grueling moments I had experienced through dusk just before I fainted. I was laid out under a bush, hiding from a sun that had scorched the skin at the top of my cheeks. I must have drifted off to sleep because, when I awoke just after sunrise, six backpackers surrounded me. Their faces looked blank in my memory but this guy in the Jimmy Cliff t-shirt was definitely one of them. I remembered his dreads from the day before, only now he had them held up with a red band. He had said, "Have some water," then, too.

I grabbed the canteen from his hand and drank from it so hard the water streamed down from the corners of my mouth.

"Slow down," he said with a smile.

I did.

"Try and breathe from your belly. Let your lungs relax."

I did that too as I looked him over.

The first thing I was taken by were his glinting green eyes and the way they mirrored the canopy of trees above. They were flecked with pops of sunlight and the colors of bark, and I reminded myself not to fall for that kind of crap again. It was the eyes that got me every time, followed closely by the chemistry, the mystery and don't even get me started on the mind. No, I, Doro Campbell was not immune to crushing. I swiftly threw up a chemistry blocker: A mental image of Dom. The way he looked at me on the Brooklyn Bridge just before we kissed for the very first time. I felt sunlight in my heart. I thought about how enveloped into our own little world I became. It was a world I was so far away from and I missed it so much.

The warm light that had filled my heart was eclipsed by reality.

I finished the water. Wound my way back into focusing on the present. "Thank you," I offered this stranger.

"De nada."

Young green grass shoots borne of the rains covered the whole ground, like an inviting wool blanket. A magical-looking mist settled around our makeshift camp and a small pot of water boiled on an Infraready burner. I had seen one these gadgets at the adventure outfitter in Lima: small, stone-colored discs the size of a teacup saucer that glowed blue when they became hot. I didn't purchase one because in no way did I think I'd be out in the wilderness for as long as I had been.

"Your oxygen levels were very low when we found you. We gave you some coca tea and an oxygen booster. Then you fell asleep and your breathing seemed to improve immediately. Mi amigos continued on but I wanted to make sure you were okay."

"Wow. I don't know what to say—"

"Say nothing."

"Well, I owe you big time."

"You owe me nothing. Human beings are meant to help each other, aren't we?"

"Sure, but *meant to do* and *actually do* are two different things."

"I am happy to see you doing better, so you see, I had something to gain."

I smiled. Not sure if I was "better" per se, but I was one step closer to Hub 48 than I was when I imagined my body toppling off a cliff.

I watched intently as this guy stirred inside the small pot with a metal wand, and then he said, "You need to eat something."

"I'm starving." I sat forward and peered into the pot. "What is that?"

"Ever tried Peruvian caviar?"

"Uhh, I'm not really a caviar person."

"It is funny because it is not caviar; it is snail."

"Funny." It wasn't funny. "No thanks."

He raised the pearl-black shell to his mouth and made an awful slurping sound as he sucked the snail out. He then closed his eyes and bowed his head to the shell before flicking it off into the grass.

"Mmmm."

He went in for another.

"That can't be good."

"In a primitive sense it is quite delicious."

I smiled. My first smile in… days? Weeks? I didn't know.

"I'll pass."

"It is very nutritious."

He pulled a steaming snail from the pot with makeshift tongs and lifted his forehead to me.

"I can't." No way.

"Come on— what's your name?"

"Doro."

"I'm Jadel."

The green-eyed guy stuck his hand out with a smile. I shook it. *Jah-del,* what a cool name. I'd never heard that before.

"You need to get energy and your strength back so we can get you back to your home. Protein, iron, your brain needs fat."

My FlexCore validated what Jadel said about food, so if snail was my only option, I would eat some snail. But I wasn't going home.

"Okay. You know what? Let me try it," I said as I cringed.

"Good choice. Now you may do like me and suck it up…"

My utter starvation was enough to keep me from gagging. My body needed food. Or maybe not— the instant I considered sucking the snail from the shell, I gagged and covered my mouth as if protecting it with the back of my sticky forearm.

"…Or you can use a little pick like the fancy people do."

"I am one hundred percent going fancy."

I took the pearl-black shell that filled the palm of my hand, along with a little twig Jadel had sharpened at the tip. I poked it into the cooked snail's shriveled, ash black flesh. I maneuvered the twig to scoop it out. It was only one bite and, who was I kidding, these snails were hardly a feast. I wished there was another way to gain sustenance but there wasn't. I had to suck it up. I closed my eyes and popped the rubbery meat into my mouth. I took one chomp and gagged, then stopped before I reached a vomit. I grabbed for the water, and washed it all down in one gulp.

"Horrendous."

"That snail just gave its life for you."

"I'd better do something important with my life then." I smiled. Jadel smiled back and nodded in agreement. Thank goodness this guy was helping me out. There was no way I would have gone into the river and caught and boiled snails on my own. I think I would have eaten my own hand off first.

"A few more of these and we can get you to the train station," he said.

"Train station?"

"Yes, you must want to get back to your home, your familia. I am sure they are worried."

I ruminated on that for a moment but then I put it back on him. "Where is home for you?"

"Me, I am always traveling. Mostly alone."

"What about your family and friends? Where are they? Don't they worry about you?"

"I keep the people in my life at a great enough distance that they never have to worry about me."

"But do you worry about them?"

"Worry is an illusion and what will be, will be. I can not stop living my life because problems *might* come up."

"I'm not exactly sure I agree. I mean, some worry is justified and you can worry and still live your life."

Jadel shrugged.

So I asked, "You're worried about me right now, aren't you?"

"I am helping you because you need it and it's the right thing to do."

I noticed a long leather cord hanging around Jadel's neck. A tiny medallion made of blue rock hung at the end of the cord with an intricate "Dm" symbol carved on it inside of an unblinking eye. I knew that symbol— from Seneca!

"Your necklace, what is that?"

Jadel looked down at the medallion.

"Oh, this I got from a place I sometimes visit."

"*A place?*"

Jadel took the Dm between his fingers. "Yes, a town. It's not too far from here actually."

My brain was inundated with so many questions in that instant that I felt like an interrogator about to unleash on a suspect, but I had to keep my cool. I couldn't scare away the one person helping me who also had a necklace with the Dm on it— an emblem that is on lapels all over Seneca.

"I want to go there. Can you take me?"

Jadel smiled. "I don't think so, it is very hard to get to."

I absolutely had to convince this guy to help me get there.

"So what, I can handle it. Try me."

"Wow, why the sudden interest in the town where I got this necklace?"

"I'm here on this trip searching for my dad. He had something just like that."

Jadel nodded inquisitively. "Why, is he missing?"

I had to tell him just enough to earn his sympathy, but not so much that he'd be freaked out by the whole thing.

"He left my family, and I just want to understand why."

Jadel looked genuinely sad for me and I could sense I was one step closer to being led to the source of the Dm necklace.

"I'm sorry," he said.

"Thanks. Jadel, I know you just met me. But you may be my only hope to help me find the place my dad could be."

Jadel seemed to be every bit as kind as he was beautiful and I couldn't imagine he would deny me this request. I mean seriously, *Jah-del*. His name rolled off my tongue in ways that I knew my name never could. He was this sweet, normal Aboves person and he was going to help me find an entrance point.

Jadel smiled and dipped his chin. He spoke softly, but that sexy rasp still came through. "Shhh. If you listen to the universe, it will tell you... oh, do you hear that?" He held his hand up to his ear and summoned in a message from out in the universe. "I can hear it say, '*Your purpose, Doro and Jadel, is to travel to the town that made this necklace, together.*'

6

I AWOKE TO the faint vibrating hum of the speeding train. I slowly lifted my numb cheek from Jadel's shoulder and straightened my stiff neck as I contemplated the fact that I had never rested my head on a shoulder like that. I tilted my ear to the left and then to the right to stretch the discomfort away. Jadel was asleep and I didn't want to wake him. He'd spent a lot of time taking care of me, with everything from hydration, to bandaging my feet, to finding me new clothes and navigating us out of the wilderness. If anyone deserved rest, it was him.

I watched Jadel breathe, admiring the stubble of a beard that had emerged overnight. I noticed I had drooled on his shirt. I was horrified and hoped he'd sleep for long enough that it would dry before he awoke.

The people across the aisle from us were a worldly looking American family: a man, a woman, and their children, a girl and a boy, both of whom appeared to be college-aged. They were playing cards. I gazed over through their window as we rode through a village alongside the sparkling browns and ochres of the Huatanay River. It was like an illustration in a children's book. I saw a black cow tied to a post, a chicken and three pigs following a woman in a long, red clay-colored dress and goggles, balancing a crate of laundry on top of her head, with a baby strapped to her back. The scenes were all very enchanting, like a window into the past. Despite the forward progress of most of the world, Peru had remained the same for centuries with the exception of the people's sun protection gear. The sky was dolphin gray with a layer of foam clouds that hushed the sun. There was no way to really know for sure how long we had been traveling. Time was elusive. My head felt like a murky, silt-filled pond and I was certain the clamminess I was experiencing all over my body was a response to being on the other side of the equator.

    I definitely didn't feel like myself down here and I wondered if maybe Reba was right when he FigureFlexed me— Had I really been hacked? If so, what did that mean for me? This wasn't some far-fetched science-fiction situation and I wasn't a cyborg as some people might believe. This was real life, and I was just a girl, albeit hardwired with super-computing capabilities. There was no way my mind could be controlled because it was still a human brain after all, and not some electronic device. I definitely felt like my thoughts were my own in that moment, and not controlled by an outside force. What could I do about it even if it had been? What would a hack really feel like? My connection to the grid was so shoddy that my Veil couldn't serve me properly anyway. I couldn't abort my mission just because my flex implant had gone wonky. This mission was *everything*. I figured I'd just avoid activating my FlexOculi altogether and keep my mindset au naturel until I could get into Seneca proper and figure things out.

Jadel began to stir, and I darted my eyes to the spot of drool on his shoulder. Oh god— it was still there.

"Buenas tardes," he said the second he opened his eyes. I could feel my face warming. "Buenas tardes."

"You alright?"

I nodded my head, felt a lump in my throat. This guy got more beautiful by the second. Especially when he smiled. Jadel took my hand. I felt excited, and guilty. Was I betraying Dom even more?

"I like you, Doro."

No matter how bad we had left things off, I still loved Dom wholly. I knew in the long run, after I had taken care of the task at hand, my goal was to get back together with him. All of this other stuff was just a test. A distraction.

"So how old are you anyway?" I asked Jadel.

"Twenty."

"Four years older than— wait a second. What's today?"

"Sixteen June," he replied.

"Oh my gosh three years older than me! I'm seventeen! Yesterday was my birthday!"

Jadel sat forward in his seat. He looked at me with big eyes and his mouth slightly agape and then he stood up.

"Friends!" He called out to the entire car with his hands up in the air.

"Jadel, what are you doing?"

He stuck his fingers in his mouth and whistled so loud I thought the windows might shatter.

"Friends! If I may have your assistance in honoring the birthday of mi amiga!"

I smiled, embarrassed, but so appreciative that he would do this for me.

Jadel looked at me with that great smile of his and began to sing, *"Happy birthday to you..."* The American family across the aisle joined in, *"...happy birthday to you, happy birthday dear—* I quickly shouted out, *"Brittany!"*

"...happy birthday to you!"

The whole train clapped for me.

I said it before and I'll say it again, Jadel was a gift. My birthday gift. I might have indeed gained an admiration for this good looking, green-eyed, dreadlocked dude, but I didn't go searching for this to happen. Down the long line of cause and effect that we were on, this was all fated to occur.

"Brittany Gilroy?" Two train attendants, one male and one

female loomed over us. Jadel looked back and forth between me and the man who spoke.

"No." Jadel said, "I am Jadel and this is—"

"Who is asking?" I interjected as I nudged Jadel with my knee.

The woman grilled me like I was a terrorist as the man spoke loud and clear enough for everyone around me to sprout blistering levels of unease. "There are some people who need to talk with Brittany Gilroy. They are awaiting our arrival at the next stop."

My stomach dropped like it did all too often since my Senecan life began. I looked at Jadel, as he twisted his puzzled gaze up to the man and asked, "Who is waiting?"

"Señor, this is confidential information. We are just the messengers." He turned to me. "But if you are not Brittany Gilroy, we have a *big* problem."

I had to buy time. "I *am* Brittany Gilroy."

"Miss Gilroy, we kindly ask that you promptly disembark the train when we arrive in La Raya."

"Okay, no problem."

This was a *huge* problem. Massive. Everything could be destroyed if S.O.I.L. figured out what I had done. Even though in that instance a million thoughts shot through my brain like high-powered lasers at a concert, what was I going to do? What would Jadel think? How much did S.O.I.L. know? Who told them? One thought I couldn't kick was, had I gotten Brittany in trouble over this? She had gone out on such a limb for me. She was the first real girlfriend I had made in Seneca. We struck a legit bond under dire circumstances, and each time after that it had only grown stronger. She shared so much and it was extremely unsettling to think she'd pay for that on my behalf.

7

WITH MY EYES closed for a second and a half tops, the entire scene raced through my mind, body and soul:

Brittany was on a Palomino and I was on a Paint. They were her two horses that lived inside the sprawling Seneca Hub 144 equine facilities. I was fortunate to receive an invite from Brittany to join her for a ride early that Sunday morning. She was trying to get her mind off of G.W. as they were on a "break." They faced uncanny pressure to stay together from their parents who saw this as an arranged marriage of sorts between two notoriously affluent families. Even though Brittany had love for G.W., they just didn't jive on that many levels. For one, she was surprisingly intellectual, and although nobody could deny G.W. was smart in his own right, he was definitely more interested in being the life of the party and showing off his quick wit to all than exercising his intellect. G.W. loved being in the spotlight while Brittany was a low-key type of girl.

"Athena likes you," she had said as she slowed down so that

we rode side-by-side. I stroked the horse's bristly neck. "I like her, too. I'm kind of realizing I'm a horse person."

"Well, you're in good company."

We both smiled. I remember thinking how incredible that place was. I wanted to absorb every ounce of it, to numb the turmoil of my mind. "This place is so beautiful. It's no wonder you come here every Sunday."

"It's my happy place."

"I can see why. I'm so glad you asked me to come. I wish you could've seen me the last time I was on a horse."

"Oh yeah, where was it?"

I smiled. Remembering the farm, the smell of Buck... but my smile vanished when my memory moved on to the storm and the mosquitoes.

"Doesn't seem like it was the most memorable experience."

"Well, memorable, yes, but not in a *good* way."

Brittany had looked at me inquisitively.

"It's a long story."

"Good thing we don't have sessions today."

Brittany was all ears.

I opened up and told her everything on that ride, short of the details of Operation Crystal. She was probably one of the best listeners I'd ever known. She didn't have any sort of reaction that made me question if telling her was the wrong thing to do. I wanted to tell her more. That Sunday morning I told her all about the bio-engineered mosquito attack on Dom and me when we were on the run from S.O.I.L., and how I woke up on Anika's farm. I just had to share all of it because I knew that if I couldn't tell her, I couldn't tell anyone. Brittany was my first real girlfriend since I'd been to Seneca and left my best friend Julie behind in the Aboves. I treasured this new friendship. The in-between period was tough and reminded me just how unfathomable life without good girlfriends was. I missed Julie terribly. I thought about her and the things we shared every day. Not just experiences, but emotions, beliefs, fears, everything. She knew nothing of what I'd been through in the last six months. I held on to the hope that one day we'd be reunited and I would tell her everything.

Brittany had that same introspective demeanor as Julie, only Julie was an artist and Brittany was a fierce advocate for animal welfare. She was an animal science scholar, specializing in equitation science. Her goal was to continue the research on preventative health measures for horses in addition to the most effective ways to treat illness and injury based on advances in science, medicine and technology. She cared for horses in a way that I could only wish all people would care for each other. I appreciated her warm heart and dedication to those innocent beasts who had no voice. It inspired me to be a better person because I knew that there was a dire need for more people like her.

"So, after all that, you decided to stay in Seneca," she said, somewhat surprised.

"Yes, well, I think you and I have a completely different set of choices, and the alternative to staying in Seneca that I was presented with wasn't something I could accept after I had learned of Seneca's existence."

"That makes perfect sense."

"And what I'm faced with now... look, I don't want to put any information on you that could get you wrapped up in this—"

"Doro, I am already so wrapped up in this. Everyone with a heartbeat is wrapped up in this in some way."

"Yeah, but, it's just so different."

"Right, but we're all connected, so at the end of the day..."

"You're absolutely right." I had hesitated but something inside of me had said, *"Tell her, tell her Doro, you must tell her now..."*

"And on the topic of connection— I know your dad goes to the South American Seneca hubs a lot, and I just found intel that my dad, who went missing three years ago, is possibly alive and living down there."

Brittany brought her horse, Prince, to a stop. It made Athena stop, too. She looked at me and put her finger over her lips as if to suggest that nothing we said in that moment was private. She turned and looked behind herself. She clicked and Prince neighed as he turned around. Athena followed.

We just rode... and I awaited her cue. I knew one was coming.

I remember wondering what had been going through her mind on that ride. I had wondered where we were headed, but trusted that it was the right direction.

We had ridden twenty minutes, across the pasture that felt much like the one I saw where we picked up Buck, only even more pristine and endless. The grass was carpet-like and in Seneca there were no such things as weeds. At least, not the nuisance type.

We arrived at a point along a mirrored wall that extended all the way across the pasture. Brittany jumped down from Prince. She came over to me and offered her hand to help me down from Athena.

She pointed her flexer to the ground and commanded, "Post." A golden post rose from the ground. She tied the horses to it with Girl Scout-like precision, never breaking her concentration. She was so stoic. She always was, with the exception of the night of the flighter crash.

Brittany looked at me as if to say, "I want to continue this conversation, but you need to stick with me." There was this incredible level of non-verbal communication passing between us. I remembered watching her shift her gaze from me to the mirrored wall that extended at least twenty stories up and then she said, "Door." As an arched doorway appeared, leading into a dark area with a subtle orange light, I knew that Brittany Gilroy was someone that I felt comfortable following into even the darkest of nights.

"Plug your nose," she whispered.

It was too late. The stench knocked me on my butt.

It was horrendous.

"I can't—" Gag. I pulled my shirt over my face.

"This is the first stage of the equine poo-renewal."

"So my telling you I thought my dad was alive made you want to bring me here? That's weird."

She laughed, and then I laughed, too. Before we knew it, the two of us shared in a small episode of uncontrollable laughter as I tucked my face into my shirt trying to avoid the all-encompassing stench of humid crap.

"I know it's weird," she said, "but this is one of the few places I know of inside this hub where there is no audio surveillance. My dad showed it to me when I was thirteen and I first arrived in Seneca. He told me this is where I should bring him or my mom if there were any secrets I ever needed to share with them. It's our safe place."

"That's how old I was when my dad went missing."

Brittany looked at me empathetically.

"Why do you think your dad is in South America?"

"Dom and I uncovered some really strong evidence that his DNA is on record as being in Colombia."

"That's crazy, Doro. My dad goes to Colombia all the time."

Brittany and I sat in a silence that spoke volumes to the scope of the potential connection between us. We didn't break eye contact, and in those soul-sharing moments I saw that she wanted to figure it all out, too. I recognized that her life was also burdened by a gigantic mystery. We were two peas in a synthetic pod that was about to be deconstructed. I realized that Brittany could be the key to the information I sought, and that I could be the key to a truth she was seeking herself. "He's got to know *something* about my dad. He has to, and if we can find out—"

"Doro, he might— you know what, he probably does, and I wish I could find out but I know how unlikely it is. My dad has the highest level of confidentiality clearance in all of Seneca. But that doesn't mean I do, too. It's been that way my entire life, and it's been for our own security. Me, my mom, and my sister."

I was bummed, but I was aware my search would not be simple.

Brittany reached for my arm. "I know it all seems fishy, but I want you to know, I know *nothing* about your dad."

"I believe you. But, Brittany, I need to find him and I think you can help."

"If there is a way I can help, Doro, I will."

I smiled. I felt deep down that she meant it. I felt it in a part of myself that I trusted even more than my logic, believe it or not.

"But I have to be upfront with you," she said. "I can't go sneaking around on my family. I have to to draw the line there. My dad may have secrets. Everyone does. But he is a good man and I already broke his trust big time with that party."

"I get that."

"But I also can't imagine what you have gone through."

"I wouldn't wish it on anyone, but this is where I am now. This is what I'm facing."

"You should go find him, Doro."

"I want to. I *need* to. I'm trying to make a plan. But the only way to do that is to go to Colombia, and as you can imagine, traversing in and out of Seneca is no walk in the park."

"Not for everyone." She offered up a genuine smile and gently took my hand. "But if you are me… you can get in and out— no questions asked."

I started to get where she was going with her line of reasoning and I liked it. Her generosity made my heart swell and my mind started to tick…

"Are you suggesting—"

"Yes. We swap facial and biometric recognition data."

After that, the rest was history. Or should I say, history in the making.

8

JADEL AND I had to get off the train before the next stop. I owed it to Brittany, I owed it to Dom, I owed it to Jadel, and I owed it to my parents because of everything they had ever sacrificed for me.

Once again, the clock was ticking. To my dismay, it never stopped ticking.

The two train attendants were clearly super cognizant of me so I couldn't make any sudden moves. My mind, however, was in overdrive, calculating options.

Jadel leaned in to whisper, "*What* was that?"

"I'll tell you when we get off this train, but there are people after me and we have to get away."

He nodded and looked at his flexer, which he kept on his arm in a metallic red band, screen-side on the inside of his wrist. "We have about ten more minutes before La Raya."

"We don't have ten minutes," I said, "I know this sounds crazy but you carry a signal flare in your backpack, don't you?"

Jadel looked at me inquisitively as he opened his backpack and pulled out a wand. I took it from him and surveyed the passengers on the train. There were two empty seats in the center of the car between us and the attendants. That was my target.

"Doro, this isn't the way."

"Jadel, this is the *only* way."

I grasped the flare. "Put your backpack on," I commanded. Jadel did. I could tell he was impressed with my assertiveness.

"What have you gotten me into?"

Tick-tock, tick-tock...

I put my backpack on as well, lifted the flare, pointed it away from my face toward the floor and twisted the cap off. I had watched my dad do this once when our family car had broken down in Joshua Tree National Park late one night. I took the back of the cap and ignited the flare like a match. The second the orange flame shot out, I tossed it into the aisle by the empty seats.

People immediately started to panic and shout. Jadel and I bolted from our seats that were two rows from the bathroom and the door that connected the cars, which opened up to the outside. Our car erupted in total chaos and the attendants' watch on us had become completely obstructed as we made a run for it.

The smell of artificial smoke filled the car and people were coughing and shouting. Jadel punched through an exit door, opening a gaping hole in the train, and tore back the panel so it was large enough for us to fit through.

Fortunately for us, the train was only doing about twenty-five miles per hour and, without any discussions as to our next move, we wasted no time and— JUMPED!

We tumbled down a hill just shy of the river's edge. I acquired a few good bruises on the way down, but nothing was broken, so up to that point I considered our escape a success. Yet I knew better than to underestimate the Seneca Observation and Intelligence League, and my money was on the fact that they would be hot on our trail.

"Doro! I had no idea you had that in you!"

"Oh, we're just getting started!" My adrenaline was cranking.

Jadel held his flexer up. "Activate compass."

He studied our position and then looked off across the tracks towards the road. I had to cut in. "Listen, I'm sure you know exactly which direction we should be going," I said, "but we need to stay hidden. There are people who are trying to stop me because they're hiding something really big and they know I'm on to them."

"From the Aboves or from—" Jadel bit his tongue. 'Where from?' is what I meant to say. Where are they from?"

That was weird.

"Did you just say *the Aboves*?" I asked.

Jadel's eyes narrowed, "Yes."

"How do you know about that?"

"The place where the necklace is from, it's below ground and they refer to the surface as the Aboves."

"What else can you tell me about this place?"

"Why don't we find safe footing and get ourselves inside before anything else, and then we can talk?"

"You're right."

Rather than taking the road, we cut up into the edge of the mountain where we were camouflaged by trees. Instead of flexing a ride, we walked for two hours in the direction towards the portal before we finally saw a car. Then, when an old, navy-colored Jeep arrived kicking up dust, Jadel ran out and threw his thumb out to hitch us a ride. The Jeep didn't stop. Over the next hour several more vehicles passed before, finally, a gas-powered Toyota Camry taxi from the turn of the century pulled over and picked us up.

9

THE HOUR AND a half taxi ride along a snaking, precarious road had me feeling woozy, but the incredible journey and anticipation of the destination kept me focused. Jadel did all the talking since he knew where we were headed and I just stared out through the taxi's dusty window at the serene blue and beige landscape studded with moody stone ruins.

I was becoming accustomed to new horizons and could only imagine what lay ahead, and moreover, what lay beneath. Especially considering this land had been roamed by humans for millennia. It was no secret to me that there was far more going on below the surface than what was happening above. If what Jadel had said was true, it could very well be that our ancestors, thousands of years ago, had prepared us for this very point in time and beyond. My senses aligned with this notion and became increasingly heightened, stomping the cloud of confusion that had consumed my consciousness into a broom closet deep inside the recesses of my mind.

We traveled across a flat valley, passing vista after vista of sublime views. Glacier capped mountains made me feel like a speck of sand along the Pacific. Santa Monica Beach felt so far away. No matter what anyone said, I could not believe that this was a small world that we inhabited. By this point, I had seen a nice slice of the globe and was convinced the saying was totally false. This world of ours was a massive puzzle piece inside infinity's labyrinth and I had emerged from a tiny little nook inside of it. This was all just the beginning of something spectacular with no end.

We had left the gray skies way behind in our dust and next thing you know the gentlest of baby blue horizons offered us an impressive welcome into the outskirts of a town called Puno.

The taxi driver cut off of the main road onto a straight and narrow but bumpy path. Everything vibrated in the car: Loose change, the knob to unroll the window, a dangling air freshener that was clearly out of scent because all I could smell were rank petroleum and corn chips. Why did all old cars reek of corn chips? Jadel leaned in to whisper in my ear, "We are directly on top of the ancient tunnels that connect the secret underground cities I am going to show you."

Jadel looked into my eyes to capture my surprise, but he was left hanging. Yes, of course I was in permanent awe with every bit of information I devoured, but my mind had already been blown to pieces back in Virginia. I forced a look of intrigue just to play the game that he was taking me to a place I couldn't even begin to imagine.

Seneca was one million percent beyond my wildest imagination. My knowledge of this secret society that existed beneath the nose of humanity only kept growing into an intricate web too far-reaching for me to fully comprehend. I wanted the whole world to know about it. Maybe together a bunch of people could piece the totality of The Seneca Society together. There *had* to be a way. It just wasn't fair. Nothing was fair, and I desperately wanted to change that. It seemed that, for as far back as recorded history went, people had been fighting for equality and justice, and this point in time was no different. But *could* it be different? Could *I* play a part in a fair and just future? I had to believe I could, otherwise why keep moving forward? I was no longer capable of finding satisfaction in scheming, gambling money, and hot-hacking flighters. Unveiling the world's truth, *our* rightful truth, was my new high.

The taxi came to a stop at the end of the dirt road where we were met by an imposing chain link fence wrapped menacingly with barbed-wire, not unlike those found encircling maximum-security prisons. Only this was in the middle of a small, peaceful valley and there were no buildings in sight.

"Gracias. Buenas tardes," Jadel said as he handed our driver a bill.

"Gracias," the driver replied quietly with a dip of his chin and a polite smile to both myself and Jadel.

I smiled back and in a flash I imagined the taxi driver's life and family. The mother he cared for, his wife working in their textile shop. Their children headed to school each morning. The more I traveled, the more nice people I met and felt connected to. They, just like everyone else on Earth, should have access to all the secret discoveries inside Seneca from the cure for cancer to large-scale cell regeneration.

In seconds the dirt road had disappeared into its surroundings. I turned my face to the sun to soak in its rays, not knowing how long it would be before I felt them again.

Peace out, Sun.

Jadel and I walked right up to the ominous-looking, towering mesh and metal fence, its top layered with jagged, razor-wire loops. These walls were intended to keep people in, not out, and posed no real challenge to the likes of us. Jadel swiftly opened his backpack and pulled out a laser knife. I feasted my eyes on the muscles tightening in his forearms as the knife's emerald-green laser sliced easily through the woven metal. Jadel bent a flap back and motioned for me to go through first. I ducked down and slithered against the ground to the other side, completely disregarding the sign in bright red that read: *Prohibido el paso!* Warning signs meant nothing to me. In fact, I started to see them as a challenge. Then I noticed something else that stood out: *Private Property of SGE Corporation. Violators will be Prosecuted—* in both English and Spanish.

SGE Corporation. SGE Corporation. Why was that so familiar?

SGE.

SGE.

Then it hit me.

Southern Gate Electric. Claytor Lake. Frank Wallingford's brother! Then there was Brittany's dad with his position and worldwide traversing capabilities that often brought him to this very neck of the woods. What was the information that connected all of this that they were hiding from us?

"Everything alright?" Jadel asked.

"Yeah, I'm fine. I was just thinking about something. Never mind, let's go."

Jadel climbed in after me and then pushed the fence back into place.

We jogged through a field of golden barley that tickled my armpits.

About a quarter mile in we stopped at a meandering stream that ran straight into a massive mound of rocks.

Jadel turned to me, "I hope you are not… how do you say, claustrófobo?"

Claustrophobia was not an option. We were too close. "I got this."

Jadel marched right into the water and I followed without

missing a beat. We trudged through the freezing cold, right up to a mound of rocks. He started up the rocks, paying particular attention to the first few that were covered in a slippery green moss. I used all my strength to hold on in case I slipped as I clambered up behind him.

Jadel stopped at the halfway point. There was a narrow space between two of the largest rocks in the center. "Mi amiga, you are about to experience a gift from the Incan people, built for us over four thousand years ago."

Jadel lifted himself up between two rocks and lowered his legs down between them.

"Follow me and be careful. It is completely black inside, just feel for the steps. They are steep yet perfect. We will climb down two kilometers and then we see again."

I found his broken yet intelligent English hot. Oh man this was a slippery slope.

Jadel sank between the rocks until all I could see were his dreads. I climbed up and watched him disappear into the tight space, barely wide enough for his shoulders if he folded his body in just a bit. I took in one last glimpse of the magnificent heights of the towering Andes and sucked in a huge breath before dropping my legs into the tiny space. I squeezed the rest of my body in all the way and then I looked up to kiss the sky goodbye.

I wiggled in behind Jadel, down into an ancient Incan stairwell made of solid stone. I pulled my goggles from my eyes to hang around my neck. We made our way, deliberately and carefully, step-by-step down what seemed like a perfect forty-five degree angle, all the while bathed in complete darkness.

"This is nuts, how did you even find this?"

"I have been exploring since I could walk, and when I was a young boy, I learned to read the iconographia on the walls of caves which led, after many other steps, to this one. As you see, it is not easy to get to."

Our voices echoed and vibrated as we descended deeper into the shaft. The sound was so cool it made me want to keep talking, but at the same time I wanted to stay quiet to hear what was happening above and below.

"When we reach the cavern, we rest," Jadel suggested.

I wasn't in the mood for rest.

10

JADEL'S ESTIMATION WAS dead-on. My quads were ready to give out as we took our final steps. We moved through a short, narrow doorway and I found myself inside a massive cavern bathed in light despite having no clear source of where all the illumination was coming from. It felt more natural than the artificial lighting inside S.E.R.C., yet we were two kilometers below ground. A mixture of large and small stone blocks that appeared to be perfectly symmetrical made up a cavernous space that was as wide as four Olympic-sized swimming pools, with walls lined with dozens of small, arched doorways.

I was rendered wrong— I thought that my mind could no longer be blown, but it was. This ancient scape was the gateway into the future. All this time I thought the ancient civilizations were only busy developing systems of farming, mathematics and language. But they knew something more, and thousands of years later, here I was, on a mission to find out for myself just what it was that they knew.

"This is just unbelievable."

"Well believe it. And we still have not made it to where we are going."

"When will we get there?"

"If I remember correctly, very soon."

I inched my way out into the center of the empty cavern, craning my neck around to take it all in. It was apparent that this place was once coated in... I ran my fingers along the wall...

"Gold," Jadel said. "The currency of the gods. Of course we know that money is power, power is money, and greed is one of the greatest detriments to humanity. Some believe that humans were left to fend for themselves as our creators retreated even deeper into the earth for the sort of heavenly life we can only hope for after death."

"And you think these doorways can lead us there?"

"I am not certain, but what I do know is that these doorways connect all of the underground cities built by the Incas. And one of these doorways, the one that we will take, goes directly below Lake Titicaca."

"Why Lake Titicaca?"

"It is Earth's highest body of water."

"So?"

Just then I heard a high-pitched sound coming from inside my eardrum.

I grabbed at both ears and tucked my head in pain.

"What's wrong?" Jadel reached for my shoulder.

"There must be something happening with my—"

I hesitated. Jadel didn't know I had a flexer implant and I knew it could potentially change his opinion of me if he knew. He was such a holistic guy, and I was what many consider to be the ultimate threat to the natural state of humans.

"Doro?"

I looked up at him and the piercing sound hit me again. My face contorted. The sound was almost paralyzing.

"Doro, what's wrong?" Jadel asked but remained calm.

I came up short of breath. It took everything in me to talk over the sound. The screeching wouldn't stop. I tried so hard to block it out. I started to think that powering up my FlexOculi and deactivating my implant might be the only way. It kept getting louder and more painful. I had to stop it and if it meant exposing my location by jumping back on the grid, then that's what I would have to do.

My screen popped up in front of me.

The sound was unbearable. I could barely see straight.

"Doro?"

"It's this excruciating sound. I have to make it stop!"

"I don't understand; I don't hear anything."

"Ahhh!" I squeezed at my head.

"We should get out of here. It could be the depth you can not handle."

"No, no…"

I didn't want to say it but we were in this together right now and I needed him to keep moving forward with me. We weren't turning around now.

"It must be coming from my… flexer implant."

I peered at Jadel through squinted eyes, ready to receive his reaction. He didn't even seem surprised, which surprised me.

"You must deactivate it."

"I'm trying—"

I closed my eyes and concentrated hard above the crushing noise assaulting my eardrums. I sent an internal activation command to my flexer for my FlexOculi to activate. The FlexOculi powered up and the screen hovered before my eyes, but the pain was almost too unbearable for me to keep my eyes open. I tried with all my might to fend off my body's reaction to the awful, penetrating sound. But the more I struggled against it, the louder it seemed to get. Something was happening, and then *boom*— "Doro."

It was a woman's voice. Super faint. I couldn't make it out.

"Yes, it's Doro! Who is this?!"

I stood up, waited for it to come again.

Jadel looked around confused, "Nobody said anything."

"It's in my head. Someone is trying to make contact."

I heard her voice again, "Doro, it's Mom."

"Mom!"

I squeezed my eyes shut. The awful sound was gone. I waited anxiously to hear her voice again. All sorts of memories of my mom raced through my consciousness, blocking out everything else.

***

My mom's face was drenched in a mixture of tears and mascara. It was exactly the way she looked that day she picked me up at the station after I had been busted in the "borrowed" flighter. It was also the same distraught look she had the day my dad's wallet was found but there were no signs of him. I knew my mom was crushed, having lost both me and my dad. Her happiness meant the world to me, so it ripped me apart as I acknowledged she might have to pay a price in order for the world to realize these hidden truths. It was something I tried to avoid thinking about, but it came to a point that I had no choice. The thoughts invaded my psyche like an army.

My mom's voice echoed through my tortured mind again. "Doro, I love you. Please come back."

I found myself in S.E.R.C. reliving that morning I first saw her when she arrived in Seneca. Over the sterile hum of air conditioning and the murmur of a few conversations in the hall, I heard the pitter patter of little Pomeranian feet. My entire body lit up. I looked past a few scholars headed back to their rooms, and there she was— my mom. We both stopped and absorbed that moment with giant smiles on our faces and joy in our hearts. I looked down to see Killer tugging ahead on his light blue woven leash.

"Killer!"

My mom let go of the leash. He charged towards me and leapt into my arms. I hugged him tight as he slathered me with his cyclone of licks and frantic squeals of delight. Tears of happiness streamed down my cheek. I looked back up to my mom, and realized that she was accompanied by Ellen. Ellen stood back with a warm smile on her face as my mom and I just soaked up the love with each other's entire beings. We were together again, in Seneca— a place where hopes and dreams become reality. At least for some, and if I have my way, one day it will be for everyone. I went to take a step forward but I couldn't move. What was happening?!

****

I was slung over a shoulder. Someone walked quickly along a gray stone path. I screamed as I flailed my body, "Mommmm, Mom! Mom!!!"

"Please, calm down."

A set of arms constricted around my abdomen. I kicked and punched but couldn't break free. "Let go of me!"

"Stop!"

All I could do to fight my way free was bite, so I chomped down on the back of the shoulder that I was draped over.

"Mierda!"

I instantly realized I knew that shoulder. It was Jadel's.

He placed me on the ground.

I was right.

"What are you doing?!" I screamed up at him. I looked around and glimpsed beside me a gigantic body of water. Crystal clear.

"Ay dios mio," Jadel grabbed his shoulder and winced in pain.

"I'm sorry! But you gotta tell me what's going on."

"You fainted. One hour ago."

He sat down next to me on the ground, "You have the bite of a cobra!"

"Well, what do you expect? I had no idea what was happening."

"I also do not know what is happening to you with your flex implant, but I think it is best to keep moving forward."

"I know, I'm sorry, Jadel. My mind is being attacked, whether or not I am on the grid. Something is happening with my implant, I can feel it. My mom was trying to connect to me. Or someone posing as my mom. I was warned that this could happen."

"Yes, the good of the flex implant— you are always connected, and the bad of the flex implant— you are always connected."

"I didn't realize that it could make me so helpless."

"I understand. I will do everything I can to protect you when these things happen, but please don't bite me again."

"Thank you. I don't know what I'd do without you here."

In fact, I didn't know why he had agreed to go to this great length for me. He looked worried and it made me worry that he would quit on me and I would be left here with no idea which way to go. He eyed me and asked, "Are you sure you would like to continue? We still have a ways to go before we reach the secret city."

I nodded emphatically. "I have to get there."

"Then we shall continue."

I smiled back. "Jadel, thank you. I have to know though, why are you doing this for me?"

"I never got to know my own father. It's the one thing in my life I wish was different. So if your father is somewhere down here in the secret city, it is my honor to help you find him. Maybe I will find some happiness in this way."

He smiled and pointed over my shoulder as if he had a gift for me. I turned to see something incredible— an enormous underground river. Glistening, clear turquoise waters flowing slowly to mysterious places beyond the scope of my sight. My mouth parted as once again the earth rendered me speechless with its raw, untouched beauty. I had only seen landscapes like these on screen and in photographs, and now they were in clear view. So intensely gorgeous, beyond my wildest dreams. How had I, and millions upon millions of others, been so lost in the concrete and metallic jungles that bastardized the Aboves that we hadn't ever truly experienced life inside the most precious parts of our planet? The levels of damage we'd inflicted had never been so apparent to me until now. I felt pissed at the people that came right before me for not taking responsibility to protect this unparalleled beauty. This had to be the atmosphere that was intended for us. Not the blaring horns of the 405, toxic landfills, radiation, pesticides and all the filth that we had created. *This* was it.

"Jadel, I don't even know what to say."

"I know. It's not often in life that we are presented with this level of beauty. It does something to us."

"I want you to know that what you're doing is extremely honorable. You ended your camping trip to help some random teenage girl find someone she loves. But I have to be honest with you, it is so much bigger than that."

"I have that impression," he replied, "And I know there is a reason that I met you."

Jadel offered me his hand and then motioned for me to step down onto a small wooden raft. There were about a dozen of them there. I wondered who, what and why, but I didn't hesitate. I carefully stepped down on the raft and he followed. There were two oars secured to either side of the raft. Jadel removed them and handed one to me. He unhooked us from the anchor we were secured to, and we pushed the raft out into the river. Either I was completely hallucinating or I was on a raft on a river several miles below the surface of the earth. Either way, it stole my breath away.

11

THE SERENITY I experienced in a time of such excruciating unknowns was magical. It was quiet, and the slow-float motion was relaxing. I wished this peace would stay with me and that I could move forward in life with this feeling until the end of time. I was surprised by the high humidity down here, because in the youth residences, where all the S.E.R.C. scholars like myself lived back in Hub 144, the climate was controlled to what I consider perfection. After several hours of floating downstream on the water, Jadel and I approached a small mouth in the river. There was a docking station that sat at the base of a stone pyramidal entryway. My heart started to beat fast at the prospect of what might unfold when we stepped off the boat.

We paddled up to the docking station and Jadel secured our raft. He stepped off onto a solid stone walkway and extended his hand out to me. As I got off the raft I scanned every inch of the monolithic structure I was inside, contemplating just how far this ancient cave and tunnel system extended. My mind was turned on by its potential marriage to our current science and technology, and more importantly, that of tomorrow. My dad believed in using every ounce of today to improve tomorrow—not for himself, but for everyone. That gutsy place inside of me that guided me along with logic was shouting at me to follow in my dad's footsteps.

"I still can't imagine how you knew to find this."

"Imagine a boy that chased information instead of girls. That deciphered ancient texts instead of man-made puzzles from the toy store. That explored the mountains and rivers instead of running around in circles in school yard playgrounds. Imagine an unquenchable desire for truth. This is what drives me forward. It is why I wake up with passion every single day."

I realized that this no-holds-barred pursuit of knowledge was Jadel's life calling, and it was meant to be that his life path and mine had intersected at this fork in the road. It gave me a great confidence in the choices I'd made thus far, even to get the flexer implant which had been giving me a run for my money recently.

I heard a sort of loud hollow thud through the archway and I cowered. "What was *that*?" Although I wanted to stay strong, fear could not be fended off that easily, considering the fact that ominous sounds off in the distance hadn't proved too sweet for me recently. But I had to remain brave because otherwise I'd just as soon admit defeat.

The sounds didn't phase Jadel. It honestly seemed that nothing did, other than when I bit him on the shoulder.

"Don't worry," he said. "Below us is the motorizada zona of the secret city, where they do digging, research and application on Doromium and other elements."

"Doromium?" Wow. "How do you know about that?"

Jadel smiled, "Active listening, attention to detail."

"What is *Doromium*?"

"It is something powerful enough that an entire secret city exists because of it. Exactly what, I can not say, but—"

"We're getting close to my dad," popped out of my mouth. I almost didn't believe it myself, but if what Jadel just said was true, my dad was most definitely here. Doromium was my dad's discovery, and if it played an integral part in Seneca, then so did my dad. This was crazy.

"How long have you been searching for him?" Jadel asked.

"He's been missing since I was thirteen."

"I am sorry to hear this."

"Thank you. Listen, Jadel, can you tell me everything you know that is going on here?"

Jadel smiled. "I will show you. But we must get inside, and be very careful."

"I seriously owe you big time."

"You owe me nothing."

"I think it's time for me to tell you that I'm going to need you to watch my back. See, I have reason to believe my conscious mind is under attack from outside forces. They don't want me to find my dad."

"Who?"

"I don't exactly know. That is why I came here alone."

"But you are not alone."

Jadel extended his arm and motioned his head towards the pyramidal entryway. An adrenaline boost forced my first step. My fingers ran along the stone, tracing the serpents and ancient scriptures carved into the rocks. In my second step I felt relief. I was astronomically closer to the truth now than several months back when I was ousted to the Aboves. In my third step I felt anticipation. What would my dad do when he laid eyes on me? He would be so proud that I found him. I longed for his approval. The absence of his pride in my life had caused a deficiency in my soul. In my fourth step the air was suctioned out of me with my first glimpse inside the belly of Hub 48.

Light shone through tubes filled with prisms that dropped down from the sky, showering me with warmth on the crown of my head. My cheeks pulled the corners of my mouth up and the rays of light calmed my anxiety. I knew it was the morning by the way the plant life all around me basked in the light that covered several hundred terraces extending up to the sky. Technologically-advanced, automated, no-soil systems embedded into ancient structures: This was just the beginning of my introduction to Hub 48, a place that was quite potentially my dad's home.

Jadel walked up to the base terrace and rubbed his fingers on a leaf, as if taken by its beauty. "Three hundred kilometers of plants."

"This is like a greenhouse on steroids!" I whispered loudly with excitement. It was stunning, but I had to keep my cool. This place got wilder and wilder. With each and every new understanding of The Seneca Society, I was falling more in love with it, and more scared of it, too.

I craned my neck to the sky and watched projected 3-D clouds roll in, releasing a light mist onto the horticulture. Then I shot my eyes to Jadel, who also reveled in the glow of it all, and I asked him, "What if someone sees us? It doesn't look like we have much of an option for taking cover here."

"I have bootlegged security clearances from my friends on the inside, so as long as we avoid the intelligence of the secret city, we will be fine."

I knew he was referring to S.O.I.L., and in my experience, avoidance of S.O.I.L. was no easy feat. I told myself, though, that without Jadel there was no way I would have found this place, let alone lived to see this day. I had to lay low deep inside the earth, and rely on this esoteric guy I'd only met a few days ago.

We made our way along to an acoustic carrier stop and hopped on for a quick ride directly into the heart of the hub.

12

AS THE DOORS opened to the central Seneca Hub 48 stop I was immediately taken by a familiar scent. Sterile, yet pure— exactly the way I recall S.E.R.C. and the youth residence sector back in Hub 144 smelling. It was totally unlike that awful ammonia they used back at my school in Culver City that probably took a fraction of a second off of my life for each breath I took of it. Although this scent took me back to my, dare I say, *home*, the people here seemed more focused. The median age must have been mid 40s, and they all seemed completely engaged in their work. Scientist and mathematician rockstars jamming out— *these* were my kind of people.

Jadel leaned in to whisper, "Let's get to a quiet space where you can wait in safety as I go find a source for a contact registry."

Completely unfamiliar with this territory, I didn't think it was a good idea for us to split up. "Don't you think we should stick together?" I asked.

"I think it is best that you stay in one secure place. If I get caught, you know your way out."

It made sense. We had totally snuck into this secret city and as far as I knew, nobody got away with that for too long. But how could I stay put when I was this close to finding my dad and understanding what Doromium meant to Seneca? Jadel didn't want this as bad as I did. He wasn't willing to risk everything to find my dad. Regardless, I followed him to one of the available private pods that I could lock myself in until he returned. Or, at least I would give Jadel the comfort of believing I would lock myself inside until he returned.

These little pods were just polar white isolation bubbles with a booth where people could step outside of the bustle for private FigureFlexes and what have you.

I slid into a seat and looked up to Jadel to feign awaiting instruction. I had to let him think he was the one driving this ship so that he would carry on and possibly return with a solution. But the mere fact that he said, *and I get caught,* raised red flags. How in the world was he going to figure this out anyway? *He* wasn't the math expert or a Senecan, so what was his plan now? *He* couldn't find the virtual back door entrances or entanglements between computer and brain. Nature was his thing and he had done us darn well with that, but I, Doro Campbell, was inside Hub 48 now, and it was time for me to do *my* thing.

He looked at me dead serious, "If I am not back by 19:00—"

"Don't say that."

We looked each other square in the eye, with him so resolute that he'd be back, and me knowing it could be the last time we ever saw each other. I couldn't put all my eggs in one basket of hope. Jadel turned to go. The clear door to the pod opened with a pleasing swoosh. As Jadel made it just deep enough into the crowd that he could no longer see me, I commanded the swooshy door to open.

I trailed him. He kept up a normal pace so as to not stand out in the crowd. I kept my eyes on his dreadlocks. It wasn't hard because he was so tall. It was so easy for me to stay in the shadows because I was only 5'4". I kept my head down, eyes up. The hallway was not unlike the city center in my hub. Actually, it was identical— down to the locations of the doorways and turns. Entrances to the acoustic carrier stops were the same, too, and that is where Jadel went. He hopped onto the carrier that was waiting there. I hopped on the car behind him and off it went.

Two stops later, Jadel got off. I silently followed, two steps behind him. He must really know this hub well to be moving around it the way he was. I definitely didn't want him to see me now, not only because he would be mad I didn't stick with our plan, but also because I wanted to see where he had clearly decided was the place to go. He was on a clear-cut mission.

Jadel suddenly turned around. I ducked behind someone and acted like I was tying my shoe. I looked back up— he was gone.

No!

I scanned every direction. No Jadel. No time to lose. Too many directions to choose from. Against my better judgement, I activated my FlexOculi. It could cut through the walls with x-ray scope and lock onto his whereabouts. Then I could find myself back on his trail. But it just kept beeping and not doing what it should. With my frustration mounting, I began to receive flex alerts. All of the alerts were contact attempts from Dom, Reba, Ellen and my mom. There were hundreds of them. My mom had tried me seventy-six times. I couldn't become distracted with that. I had to find Jadel. I couldn't let the disturbances from back home squash my shot at finding my dad. I was too close. This moment was everything. Nothing could mess me up! But I couldn't control the inundation of flexes and FigureFlex requests.

My FigureFlex mom stood in front of me, holding Killer in her arms.

Doro, You are not safe! Please flex me immediately. We are all so worried about you. You have to come home. Please, Doro—

Jadel was getting farther and farther away. I smashed my hand into the air button to close out my mom's flex. I couldn't let incoming noise drown out my rational thought. Blocking my mom out felt horrendous, but she had it all wrong. The fact that she was being manipulated to say those things killed me. Because of that I was forced to keep her away. I couldn't tell her that they were doing this to us. Why couldn't they just let us be? Especially my mom. She'd been through a never-ending emotional hurricane and I just wanted it to end.

I knew my state. I was fine. I shed the dead weight, turned off flex alerts, and got down to business, knowing very well they could potentially be on to me now, tracing me through my flexer that was now connected back to the grid. I had to find cover stat and then handle that vulnerability. I booked it down the hall, peering in every direction, trying to go incognito as my FlexOculi scanned every single face. Finally, as I passed a closed golden door, the sensor went off: Jadel was on the other side. I stopped, made my way to lean up against the wall right next to it.

I activated a new flex device I had installed before we left: The X-scope. It could see and hear through up to two feet of any sort of matter with the exception of lead. A 3D geogram of Jadel and two other people appeared on my FlexOculi monitor, letting me see them in graphic lines that were constructed by heat sensors. But the audio was shoddy. I moved along the door to try for better reception but I couldn't make out what they were saying— there was way too much static for some reason. It was like someone he was with had blockers running on their flexers. That was the only explanation. I'd tested this stuff with Reba before I left. This made me suspicious. Oh my gosh. It suddenly hit me, was it Jadel? Did *Jadel* have an implant? That would be nuts, but it would explain so much. He had known I should deactivate mine and he didn't even react to the fact that I had one. But why wouldn't he have told me *he* had one when *I* told him? Who were these people, how did he know them, and why didn't he tell me he'd be in contact with people he knew down here? Jadel had people inside Seneca. Was he secretly a traverser? Who was this guy?

I could tell by their geogram body language that they were about to leave the room. I ducked behind someone just as the golden door opened and they emerged. Jadel came out first. I watched him head back in the direction he'd come from and I knew I had to think quick, but first I had to see the two people that came out behind him and capture their identity. Out they came— two men in black. Oh my god: S.O.I.L. One of my legs started to shake, but I kept it together in the face of one heck of a betrayal that I did not see coming. Jadel was with S.O.I.L. This was a trap!

My game plan was null and void now. The sudden revelation that Jadel was in contact with S.O.I.L. knocked the wind out of me. What a masterful deception, posing as some pure-hearted, outdoorsy type, when in fact he had direct ties to the most untrustworthy group I'd ever come across.

There was no time to throw myself a pity party. I had to let go of my interest in Jadel and make my next move with him in my wake. I flex-grabbed the identities of the S.O.I.L. agents so that when I came across them in the future, I'd have them locked in.

S.O.I.L. knew I was in Hub 48, and I was back to rolling solo. I needed to hop on the grid with Brittany's identity and download the maps to this foreign hub. Then I could locate and search the research labs and ask around to some of the real science types that I could envision working with my dad.

Although S.O.I.L. was obviously onto the fact that I was maneuvering through the Senecan city as Brittany, I couldn't imagine they'd have shut down her grid access. I'd bet they were still using it to try and find me. First things first, I had to re-code Brittany's location settings to scramble across the entire hub. So I cloned her recognition data and attached it to dozens of people around me that headed in every direction. S.O.I.L. would know I was here, but not exactly where, because as far as data was concerned, Brittany was all over the place now. To err on the side of caution, I had to be ready to make it as far away as possible from this spot within *milliseconds* of completing this operation.

13

THE MAP OF Hub 48 hovered in front of my face. I had a bird's-eye view of the city sector that contained all the leisure spots like the shopping, restaurant, and fitness districts. This is where I was located, which was indicated by a blinking white light. I concentrated hard and pulled out even further to surf across the other sectors. It was a lot to take in, but getting my bearings straight had to happen immediately because I was on borrowed time and the only weapon I had was my mind.

    Hub 48 was a giant hexagon with an entrance to each of the six sectors on every one it's six sides. Hub 48 was also connected to two other hexagons— one was the agriculture zone and the other was called the dynamo zone. I had no clue what the dynamo zone was, but I absolutely wanted to know. Regardless, it appeared that Hub 48 was much more expansive than Hub144. The acoustic carrier encircled the Hub 48 hexagon with a stop at each sector entrance (City, S.E.R.C., Residences, Facilities & Operations, S.O.I.L., and X) and direct lines from each one into the center of the hexagon, where there was a square. The square was one hundred thousand acres and labeled S.I.C.E. I honed in to read: Seneca Inner Core Exploration. Working population: 80,000.

Knowing that my dad had been collaborating with the world's largest particle research lab in Switzerland in the years before his disappearance, it made sense that he'd be one of the eighty thousand inside S.I.C.E. He'd often said that everything we needed to make the planet function optimally was just below our feet, but somehow that type of research never scored anywhere near the same kind of funding or attention that space exploration got. Well, it was pretty obvious to me that right here and right now in Hub 48 there was an insane amount of money spent and effort made to explore what was right beneath us.

The clues were just too obvious to ignore. Knowing what I did about my dad's life passion, there was no doubt in my mind that he was here, doing the work he loved. I felt punched in the gut to think that he had given up on me and my mom for this… that he'd rather spend his days in the headiest of science experiments than in the little ones we used to do in our own backyard. I shook off the feeling of abandonment and pulled myself together. There was a reason I was here. I reminded myself that nothing was as it seemed. Assumptions did not equate to truth. My dad loved me. I loved him. That was the only truth I had to go on, and the fact of the matter was I didn't know my dad's truth. It could very well be that he thought he would eventually be able to bring my mom and me here, just as I thought I would find a way to get my mom inside when I made the decision to join The Seneca Society.

With my head down, eyes up, I slid along with the crowd, taking in the expression on every face in my path. There was no telling who would try and grab my facial recognition. There was a pretty calm vibe in this city center at dinnertime. I was running on empty, however. The smells emanating from the restaurant district reached my nose. My stomach grumbled, pleading with me to make a pit stop, but I'd have to move forward on fumes. Some sort of power bar would do the trick once I knew I was out of the red zone, where I was prey being hunted in S.O.I.L.'s wide open field. The reality was there was no telling when I would be safe again, I just had to keep moving.

I walked several blocks to the entrance point through which I had come into this hub with Jadel. I hopped on the acoustic carrier and took a seat in the corner for a ride to the center of the hexagon. I kept my head down with a heightened awareness of any movement around me. I thought about Jadel on that ride, and wondered what he had planned for me. What would have become of me if I had waited back in that pod for him?

I reached the stop at one of the six entrance points to S.I.C.E. I took a mega breath and prepared myself for the next phase of my search. An adrenaline rush kicked in the second my foot hit the ground inside S.I.C.E., but I also instantly had the sensation that

I was being followed. I could have easily chalked it up to paranoia, but this was no time to snooze on my intuition. It was hard to dialogue with my body's warning signs at this particular point in time because I was transfixed by the magnificent, endless vortex of metal and lights in front of me. Stainless steel pipes, intricate tubing that went on and on, walkways stacked on top of more and more gray metal walkways, and systems of yellow ladders built in a perfect architectural pattern. There were men in blue, but also black, and all white, masked, behind clear-coated walls. Rooms ablaze in blasts of polar white steam. Tanks of glowing magenta liquids, flowing, bubbling, gushing. A group working in one room engulfed in blue lights wore what looked like space gear. This was excruciatingly beautiful in a totally geeked-out kind of way and the acoustics were a calming bath of sound.

We humans have come a long way from the Bunsen burners that my dad used when he was a kid. I bounced between feasting my eyes on this place, watching my back, and making justifications for the choices my dad had made— well, the choices I wasn't even sure that he actually made. It was impossible to stifle the assumptions. It was impossible to ignore my twice— no— *thrice*— shattered heart.

I made my way inside and blended in to become another mouse in a functional maze. My sights were set on finding a relaxed, unassuming type of individual, and asking them to locate my dad based on his Senecan ID, which I had secretly locked in my Veil during Operation Crystal. This meant I'd have to hop back on the grid to access it, and of course I'd have to deal with any of the noise that would come with that. In the midst of my thought processing I had been spotted. Ten feet in front of me stood four masked men in black.

Uh-oh: S.O.I.L.

"Don't move!"

Screw that— time to move at lightning speed. I darted for the closest yellow ladder and scrambled up it. It shot fifty feet up to a walkway. I hauled it, not looking back.

"Stop!" a young guy shouted. His voice hit me hard. It sounded almost familiar. I hesitated, gulped, but kept moving. I heard their storming feet right behind me. Climbing the ladder, I felt the vibration in the metal. Heart pounding, I was almost at the top.

"You don't want to do this!" the guy yelled again. Then a woman yelled, too, "Doro!"

I kept my eyes on the steps in front of me. I didn't want to look back and trip up. I couldn't let them gain footing on me, but hearing my name like that made me instinctively turn around. Why was she calling my name?

I was so high up now. The scene below me was terrifying. Some people in lab coats looked on, but cleared out of my way as I got up onto the hanging footpath and sprinted across at full speed.

The electricity surging through my blood compounded in one millisecond when I saw Jadel and two men in black coming from the other direction down the footpath. Jadel himself was in black. Jadel wasn't just in cahoots with S.O.I.L., Jadel *was* S.O.I.L.! I didn't know which way to turn. S.O.I.L. was after me from both directions. I looked up and jumped to hang on to the wall above me. I scaled it and climbed up another level. Then I started back in the direction I'd come from, faster than I'd ever run in my life, when BAM— my feet were grabbed. I hit the floor hard, my chin took the brunt of the fall. Blood started gushing from my tongue that was almost bitten off at the tip.

"Ahhh!" I shouted. I looked down at my feet locked in by a leg cuff drone. I had to keep moving, but I couldn't use my legs. The four masked S.O.I.L. agents rushed up on me—

"Get away!" I screamed, even though I knew they wouldn't, but it just came out of my mouth.

"Relax!" one guy said, and another one chimed in, "We're on the same side!"

"The hell we are!"

I saw Jadel climb up onto the path we were on.

"Doro!" he shouted.

"Jadel, you—"

The masked S.O.I.L. agent threw a gag in my mouth so I couldn't speak! I gasped through my nose, pushed out moans of anger from my gut.

As the masked guy turned back to Jadel who had a stun gun lifted on us, he popped one off on Jadel— it caught him in the shoulder. He dropped. "Don't make me stun you too!" the man with the stun gun barked at me.

Jadel's two accomplices climbed up with their stunners, too, but POP— POP!

Jadel's accomplices dropped just like that. My mind was blown. What the hell was happening?! S.O.I.L. versus S.O.I.L?!

The masked guy swiftly pulled a clear plastic box full of needles and syringes from inside his pocket, ran up to Jadel and the other two men on the ground and injected them. I looked at Jadel like *take that sucker*, but also felt a bit of guilt. We had an undeniable connection. There was no way he was one hundred percent out to get me. How could he have nursed me back to health, referred to me as his amiga, and then wished me captured by bad guys?

None of this made sense. Actually, I am certain Jadel saved my life. I wouldn't be this close to my dad without him, even if he had something else going on. But now he was being shot up with god-knows-what and I was just watching and not doing a thing. I started praying that I wouldn't get a shot because I knew full well what shots meant in Seneca and they certainly were not for the flu.

The other masked agent strapped me to his chest and the four of them activated the jet packs on their backs and blasted off from the footpath! We flew through the center of S.I.C.E. with literally every eye in the place on us. My mouth gagged, my feet trapped. Here we go again.

14

WE DESCENDED A wall in an upper corner of the facility. One of the men in masks knew where we were going and the other three stayed behind him, with me and my guy bringing up the rear. I use the term *my guy* loosely. I was going to ditch this fool as soon as I had the chance. I tried to brainstorm ways to escape, but four on one? This was going to be tough.

The man in the lead spoke with a South American accent, but I couldn't identify where exactly he was from because, aside from Peru, I'd never been down here. If I could hop on the grid, my flexer would let me know the origin of his accent. Alas, I could not risk that right now.

His voice shook a little. "We're in the clear for… possibly only seconds." Then my guy said to me, "I'm really sorry about the gag." I recognized his voice. I was instantly relieved, but shocked with myself for being so oblivious.

As we cruised through the open space he unstrapped the gag.

"Reba?!"

"I'm sorry, Campbella, we couldn't risk you talking—"

I was instantly relieved it was him, but then I snapped back to reality, upset and confused. "You scared the crap out of me!"

"Shhh. If we get busted, this whole thing is over."

"Who is *we*?!"

Reba stayed calm and quiet.

"Who, Reba?! Tell me!" My body fidgeted hardcore from the surging adrenaline and desire to break free, but I was strapped in so tight there was no way I was going anywhere, and if I broke loose, I would drop, and if I dropped, I was dead.

"Just stay chill. I'll explain everything soon," Reba assured me.

This whole situation was horrendous, but I obliged and stayed quiet. I felt so constrained and blown away by this sabotage inflicted by my supposed closest friend. I looked at the other guys in black. Who were they? Dom? One had to be Dom! And whoever else could be with them? Ellen?

In an unsuccessful attempt to get my nerves in check, I clamped down on my lips and tightened my jaw, almost cracking my back teeth. I was so close to finding my dad and the truth of this entire society, and now everything was thrown off track.

All this time I'd thought that my friends and I wanted the same thing: to find and expose the corruption inside Seneca, but now I just didn't know. Why would Reba have come here after all this time? And Dom— I don't think I knew it was possible to love and hate one person so much. He crushed my heart and he made it gush, but right I was too entangled in the chaos to pay attention to my meddling heart.

We came to a stop.

The South American S.O.I.L. agent commanded a door to open. We moved swiftly through it. The door closed behind us. We were inside a tiny, dimly lit room. There was a very slight, almost undetectable vibration in this space. Nobody spoke as we continued on through a solid stone tunnel for about twenty more yards. My ankle cuffs had wheels so I was rolled along, still strapped to Reba. I started to feel a calm settle over me, like after an intense vomit or a big cry. Then my mind came charging its way back in to remind me that I am not safe until I am in control.

The end of the tunnel opened into a labyrinth of tubing encasing more tubing, turquoise water cooling smaller pipes of colorful liquids. It was so quiet it was almost peaceful. Then the masks came off: Reba, Dom, Anika! And some scruffy skinny dude with dusty red hair, freckles and a Spanish accent. Maybe in his late-twenties.

Dom hurried right up to me, unlatched my drone cuffs and embraced me. He held on tight. His hard breath was all I could hear.

"You have no idea how relieved I am," he exclaimed, with his arms around me. My arms hung at my sides, frozen between the choice of pushing him away and hugging him back. The others watched us intently and I couldn't help but wonder what everyone's motivation was.

"Relief?" I hissed. "What are you all thinking?! Should I be relieved that S.O.I.L. has us on their radar now because of this?"

Reba snapped, "You think that is something new? We're always on S.O.I.L.'s radar!"

He had a point. But I was pissed.

"I know, Reba! So you should know how crucial it is to stay one step ahead."

"Of course I do! We all do!"

"Then you must have a real good reason for stopping me!"

Anika came in close and spoke like this was the most important matter of all time, but she was also as centered as a monk. "Doro, what the guys have been trying to tell you is all true. If we don't wipe out the virus in your implant," Anika said as she shook her head in distress, "we're going to lose the Doro we all know and love. There is no better reason than that."

That hit me like a punch in the stomach. I shot my gaze to the stranger. "Who are *you*?"

"Don't worry about *me*. These people risk their lives for you, and I don't even know you, but because Reba vouched for you, I am here, risking my life, which is something I am *really* starting to regret."

This guy was authentic. I looked at Dom, Reba and Anika. They all looked back at me as if to say, "Of course this guy is authentic, and you need to listen to us."

Then Reba explained, "This is Giancarlo. He lives here in Hub 48 and he's an Intuerian, too."

"So what's he doing here?"

He didn't like my tone. "How about not talking about him like he's not here," Giancarlo snapped back, "when *he* is responsible for sneaking your friends in here under the guise of the Intuerian diplomacy program."

Reba interjected, "He put his life in Seneca on the line for me so that I could save my friend, and *we* could find the way together."

I tried to collect my thoughts. Despite the paralyzing uncertainty, I felt a mounting desire to quell my paranoia and accept what they'd been telling me. It felt like the right thing to do. Just let everything go and let the people in my life who had my back before get my back again. Why was this so confusing? Maybe I *was* messed up. It totally made sense that my brain was under siege. I had trusted a stranger in the wilderness, but not the people who knew me best. That wasn't me.

Dom spoke with a tremble in his voice. "Doro, not coming with you is the biggest regret of my life. I reacted because I was hurt and I realize I wasn't just putting you at risk, I was turning my back on everyone, including all my loved ones in the Aboves. We all know too much to just sit back and let this unravel in a way that isn't for the greater good."

It felt so incredibly good to hear him say these things. *We* knew how huge this was. Way bigger than us. We needed to unify. I was petrified. If I didn't let him back in, I could lose him again. I deeply wanted my team to fall back into alignment. Dom could tell I was beaten down. "Doro, you and I can take things slow," he said, "but we all need to hurry up and find your dad."

Anika looked to me and, although she was quiet, she spoke with such certainty that I had no choice but to actively listen. I felt confident with this woman's intentions in life and she most definitely did not have any reason to betray me. "Sweetheart, we need to reboot your internal flex system."

I looked to Reba. "We don't have time."

"We don't have any other choice, Doro, you've been compromised—"

"How? Can you prove it or are you just assuming?"

He scrunched his lips and furrowed his brow in response to me. He knew that I knew it was true.

I turned back to Anika, to which she replied, "All sorts of ways. This is a hack with purpose— disorient and distract. I'm sure you're seeing visuals of things that aren't actually there. For example, they'll make poison look like water when you are dying of thirst. Or they'll send a vicious dog running out in front of you when you're about to turn in a certain direction."

"The watermelon," I mumbled to myself, and then louder, "I fell off a cliff!"

"Exactly, you see, and another, even more dangerous part of this hack stimulates the parts of your brain that are responsible for certain emotions like fear and paranoia. By triggering certain brain signals, they can lead you to become legally insane, to the point of no return."

I was defeated. I never imagined that my greatest strength could be manhandled like this, but the proof was in the pudding, and my brain was that pudding.

"As long as you are on the grid, you will be inundated with misinformation," Anika said.

"I'm off now, at least I think I am."

"So then you must have noticed something was going on."

I did, and it clicked. I looked at my friends. I'd resisted them so badly that part of me wanted to just say *no* for the sake of not looking like an imploding jerk. Staying inside my cocoon was safer and much more in line with my character.

"Yes," my voice trembled. I knew there was something fiddling around inside my mind, making me weak. Something I couldn't control.

"Campbella, a weak person never would have made it this far," Reba said, flashing his big brown puppy dog eyes. It felt like an old friend coming home. Or like when Killer darted across Washington Boulevard in rush hour traffic and someone stopped their car and jumped out to pick him up. He was safe. I didn't feel much relief like that these days.

"I'm sorry, Reba."

I had totally shut him out. He never did that to me. I kept doing it. This had to stop. He couldn't have been more forgiving. "Don't apologize. I fully understand what you're up against because in many ways I have felt your pain all along the way."

Dom pulled his backpack off and unzipped the top. He carefully removed a silver mask from it and handed it to Anika.

Reba tapped me on the shoulder. "Giancarlo and I are going to keep a lookout. We'll be back soon."

I nodded, knowing how risky all of this was, for all of us. Giancarlo's face was awash with strong annoyance. This all had to work out for everyone who ever did anything for me. But not just my people, for all people who put others in front of themselves. The giving, thoughtful people— they fuel me.

I took both of Reba's hands and held them tight as my hands shook. I looked to Giancarlo and back to Reba. "Be careful."

15

MY MIND WAS flooded with a million thoughts a second. A wicked sense of fear tried to sneak its way in as I lay still in the pitch black, but I was aware of who was with me: Dom and Anika. The last time the two of them were together at my side incredible things happened. It was different this time. We were not in the secret medical chamber on Anika's pastoral farm in the Virginia countryside where she had successfully performed the flex implant procedures on me and Dom. We were inside a highly-secretive subterranean city in a foreign country, and I was basically maneuvering through it as an enemy of the state, with a group of accomplices— a scenario not exactly on my to-do list when I started high school. I had no doubt that we were high on S.O.I.L.'s radar. But radars were meant to be avoided. Better yet, rendered obsolete.

My body lay flat like a log against the chilled stone ground. I was far enough detached from my body and deep enough inside my mind that the cold didn't bother me nearly as much as it usually did. The mask strapped to my face formed a suction through which no air could seep in. Concerns ping-ponged all over my neural circuits, but the second the red laser light fluttered across my eyeballs, not another thought crossed my mind. An intense orchestra of lights kicked in. There was no telling what was happening, but I didn't think about it. I just waited in paralysis as the laser lights checked me back to the baseline.

For something that wreaked such havoc inside of me, the fix was super quick. The first thing I felt was a tingling in my toes. I wiggled them. Then I did the same with my fingers, only to realize my hand was being held. I didn't have to see to know who it was. The electricity between us awakened my senses. After all the time I spent getting beaten down by the elements in the wilderness, I didn't think it was possible to feel this way ever again. I was grateful that my friends had come for me and got me back to this point.

I felt a gentle tap on my forearm and Anika calmly said, "I am going to remove the mask now. Just take it easy, no sudden movements as your brain reconnects with the rest of you."

"Okay."

My mask came off. Anika and Dom were right there. The massive weight was lifted as the cloud that enveloped my head was gone. I didn't even realize how bad it had been until it was gone. I let the moment sink in while avoiding thinking about what I knew had to happen next.

I saw Dom's smile and the twinkle in his eye and just like that, for a moment, everything felt alright. I reached up and ran my fingers through his hair and down the stubble of his sideburns to his jaw line. He leaned into my hand and looked at me the way I'd missed hardcore. His eyes said *I love you*. His eyes said *I care about you*. His eyes said *no matter what I am yours*. The feel-goods rushed through my whole body and I think he felt it too but he just seemed so pensive. "I haven't been able to find it in me to get any sleep or even go for a haircut since you've been gone," he quietly said.

"Honestly, Dom, I have no idea how much sleep I've had, or not had, or even how long it has been since I saw you last."

"Twenty-seven days," he said with absolute certainty.

He could have said a week, he could have said a year, but no matter how long it was it was too long and I was just glad that period of time was over.

"Thank you for not giving up on me," I said as I caressed his hand.

He looked like he was about to cry underneath his warm, trembling smile. "I thought about you day in, day out," he whispered in my ear. "It killed me that I couldn't be with you on your birthday, but I got you this, and I couldn't wait for the moment that I could give it to you."

Dom unzipped his jacket and reached inside to pull out a little black satchel from his pocket. I slowly sat up as he held up the most beautiful necklace I'd ever seen. He gently placed the delicate gold chain that had a teardrop-shaped pearly moonstone with a baby-blue shimmer, around my neck. I looked down at it and then up to his sweet eyes and kissed his full lips.

I tucked my arms up under his and rested my head into the nook. Soothing was an understatement. I rubbed my thumb on the stone. This gift brought me right back to the Brooklyn Bridge and that deep connection I had with Dom. Against all the odds, we were back together again like a magnetic force.

Anika stayed quiet and still, like she was meditating and letting Dom and I build up our psychological immune systems for what was ahead. I was really taken by the fact that Anika was even here because I knew where she'd come from and whom she'd left behind to be here. She had sacrificed so much, and I didn't know what I had done to deserve that. "Anika, you have done so much for us."

"Oh, Doro, you and Dom have done more for me than you'll ever know."

"Us?" I asked, thinking that we had been the ones getting all the help and not the other way around.

"Yes," she said. "You've helped me find purpose again. And I will not let that fall by the wayside. Just *being* is no longer an option for this old lady. I know what we are on the brink of here."

I was definitely in good hands. But I also had to bring my A-game with no delay, because these loved ones of mine were *my* responsibility now. I'd brought them into this.

Dom agreed, "We all know how important this is, and nothing will compromise that ever again. I sent Reba a flex. As soon as he's back with Giancarlo, we'll hit it. I can't wait to shake your dad's hand, Doro."

I could not wait for that either.

16

TWENTY MINUTES AFTER my reboot, a couple of quinoa bars, and a nutrient shot, I was feeling light as a feather and sharp as a samurai sword. Stepping inside the central foyer to S.I.C.E. I could tell that the blisters had healed and my feet weren't in as much pain as they had been the past few days. I was accompanied by a very strong garlic and sun-dried tomato aftertaste that had no expiration date. For that I felt bad for my accomplices, but I chose to be selfish and relish in the medicinal culinary bliss. It was something I more than missed. My senses were tickled just by being under this massive dome of glowing butterscotch light that soared high above the trees and gleeful birds, covering several miles.

Thousands of individuals in every shade of life were walking along with purpose. All about us were coffee and snack stands, media posts with multilingual B3 broadcasts and hallways shooting off in every direction.

I noticed that one of the screens had Becky Hudson on it, so I motioned for the others to come check it out with me as I knew she was on the English speaking station and I hadn't caught up on any Senecan news in ages. It hit me that it would be good to stop and take a dose of world happenings real quick before I resumed this tunnel vision to finding my dad. As we approached the monitor, behind Becky Hudson there was a shot of the Pope getting off of a private BoomJet on a tarmac and waving to the people below.

"*Pope Francis Notaro has been in Geneva for two days, ending his visit before the United Nations with an address on the global spiritual crisis of flex implants.*"

Images of people in zombie-like states in mental hospitals, being strapped down, looting stores and crashing cars, flashed on the screen.

"*The Pope has called upon the citizens of the world to renew our commitment to our God by not playing God. He stressed that for Catholics and non-Catholics alike it is imperative that we put our faith in our respective deities rather than playing God on our own. And implanting computers into our physical bodies is just that. He said without any hesitation that there is no greater form of blasphemy.*"

Dom and I looked at one another and then to Anika. She had a slightly different interpretation of what the flex implant meant in the religious landscape. "Science and religion have butted heads for a long, long time. Don't let that report fill your head with stuff that isn't necessarily the absolute truth."

Dom was not sold. "I don't know, Anika. Doesn't it scare you to say something like that?"

"It never scares me to say what I think."

"Yeah, well, it's hard to refute the word of the Pope."

"I respect that," she said, "but what if you had hard evidence to the contrary?"

"Then we'd be having a different conversation. I just think it's convenient for us to believe these flex implants are harmless and we are without sin by engaging with what they can do. I've seen what can happen. It's like we've opened Pandora's box."

Dom was right on with that. The flex implant was a vehicle for both good and evil, some of which people might not be able to control once they had one.

"This is true," Anika conceded.

Giancarlo just had to chime in. "I think you're being dramatic, you Americans. Everything is over-thought and over-talked. A hundred years ago they had the same debate about tattoos. Whether it was artistic expression or ruining the body God gave you."

With that, Dom lightened it up. "Well, at least my parents won't ever know that I did this like they would if I had a tattoo. My mom is so proud of my baptism pictures."

Anika and Dom's mom go way back. "Your mom would be so proud of the man you are becoming, Dominic. Don't let a news broadcast on some antiquated interpretation of God's word lead you to believe otherwise."

Reba weighed in, "I agree, Dom. A flex implant is just like a drug. It can be used for good, or it can be abused. The device itself doesn't define your soul. It's all about how you exercise your free will with the capabilities the device provides you."

Dom reached for Reba's hand and shook it. "Thanks, man."

Anika offered her support, too. "He's right. The people we just watched going crazy on the news were probably using the implant for all the wrong reasons, if they even had the implant at all."

Dom shrugged with his hands up. "We don't even know that though. Because, as we've learned, it makes even the smartest people in the world vulnerable to malicious intentions."

Regret was written all over Reba's face for the decision I had made to get the implant. He didn't have to say a thing and I could tell he didn't want to. I understood Reba's nerves, but I wasn't here to dwell on the past or question my decisions. I was ready to rock the future. "We're only vulnerable if we stay stagnant, and that isn't me. It's time for us to do what we came here for."

Looking around at the others, I could feel my motivation rise like a fever. I could see it happening in them, too. Giancarlo was fidgety, though, nervously scratching his chin and stretching his neck. I was starting to learn that he always did that. He attempted to calm himself by taking both hands and rubbing the temples on either side of his forehead with his eyes closed. I could tell he wasn't a fan of mine, but he knew deep down that assisting on this path that I was at the center of was the right thing to do. Because he felt that, and Reba felt that, because *two* Intuerians believed in me, my drive was on fire.

S.I.C.E. was like a college campus and research center set in the future. An electric energy surged between conversing groups of scholars and scientists whose endeavors were supported by resources of the highest caliber. The bustle of brilliant minds working together like this was sublime. Being in their midst, I could feel the extraordinary level of information flowing through the veins of this place.

We all donned new blue gear that Giancarlo got for us. Although I knew there was no such thing as being perfectly invisible in Seneca, this kept us camouflaged in the pack. I also kept a knit hat pulled down just over my eyebrows and my hair tucked up inside of it. While Dom and Giancarlo stayed in the lead, Reba and Anika were on either side of me as though they were carrying me inside a human shield.

My FlexOculi was fired up. As we moved through the space, I ran a little program I wrote that grabbed everyone's Senecan ID and showed me who they were the moment I looked at them. It was a diverse bunch down here in Hub 48 and that was cool to see, but not one of the thirty I scanned so far was my dad. My one in eighty thousand chance of finding him doing it this way was super lame. It was time to fix the odds.

Giancarlo had come back with the current work location for the Senecan ID that contained my father's DNA and so it was in that direction that we headed. Giancarlo knew exactly where we were going. We took one of the countless hallways I had peeped into on my way in. The only obstacle on the horizon was getting into the highly secured "Dm sector" in the heart of S.I.C.E. I prepared to hijack recognition data for five individuals that came out of the Dm sector in order for us to get in under their information. I was aware this was an intrusion of their privacy, for me to use my flex implant to hack into their Veils and copy their data, but it was the most foolproof way I knew of in the moment. She who hesitates finishes last, and I wasn't about to let that happen.

As I took my position against the wall near the laser entrance, Dom, Anika, Reba and Giancarlo stayed on patrol for any suspicious looking characters. In just a few moments I assigned us the flex recognition data from five unique individuals. I wouldn't be surprised if those individuals were some of the top scientists alive, but as smart as they were, they were totally oblivious to my hack. As my friends and I walked around, we would emit signals as if we were those scientists, and that gave us clout as far as sensors-to-let-us-pass-through-doors goes.

"Psst." I signaled my friends. They hustled over and we

walked in as if we were supposed to. This time I took the lead. Something pushed me to. That something was that reassuring Intuerian vibe from Reba and Giancarlo. It spoke volumes to see that they had no worry on their faces, but rather excitement. Everyone did. We were a team that would have made Amerigo Vespucci proud.

17

THE VARIOUS SENECA hubs did bear striking architectural and functional similarities to one another, but the differentiation between sectors and the many zones inside each one continued to astonish me. We made our way through a light blue, illuminated stone-dome walkway that opened into a whole new world.

A massive plexiglass cylinder filled with electric blue liquid that flowed upward was at the center of this expansive area. The cylinder plunged deeper down into the earth, and soared higher up than we could see. The surrounding extensions of hundreds, if not thousands, of tubes, tunnels and rooms coming off of the cylinder demonstrated an unbelievable amount of thought and innovation. So much effort and progress had to happen to get us to this point in our existence. I think it blew me away more than usual because this wasn't just some vast underground farming set-up, or a poo-renew system, or even the best sushi of all time, this was a testament to the immeasurable ingenuity of the human mind. The experiment before us was beyond the likeness or scope of anything I'd ever seen or read about. They're still spewing the fallacy of Christopher Colombus in schools in the Aboves when what kids really should be learning about is *this*. What was going on here? It had to be huge.

Dom took my hand. "I am so grateful that we are here seeing this, together."

"I know," I said. "We are so close, Dom. I can feel it."

We spoke to each other but, for once, without looking at one other. We held hands and marveled at the beautiful liquid in front of us. I felt my face soaking it in, glowing. The blue was so transfixing. Blue signified hope, trust and purity. It usually calmed me, but right now there was too much electricity in my blood.

I looked at the others and they, too, were moved by this place. Wordlessly, we wound our way in past huge open doors of skyscraper-sized projects. I brought up the rear as I was enraptured by what I saw through one plexiglass wall: a piece of machinery that must have weighed thousands of tons and was so intricately built it had to have taken decades to make. With each step I took, and each display of science and technological glory I passed, I was becoming acquainted with my dad's wonderland.

I suddenly and unexpectedly got choked up. I stopped walking to pull it all in and absorb the possibilities. That this may be a life my dad had chosen over the one with me and my mom. He could have been given the same choice as me, and I could imagine him not being able to say no to this.

My neck was suddenly grabbed and my mouth cupped shut by a hand. I couldn't move and I couldn't scream in this suffocating hold. Ripples of adrenaline shot through me. My eyes popped wide and my nostrils flared for air. I was used to outsmarting people with my mind but I had yet to become accustomed to physical attacks. This had to be S.O.I.L. The unknown possibilities of what they would do to me this time around was terrifying. The attacker moved his face right next to mine and each time his breath hit my cheekbone, the tension inside me flared. My hands were cold but my feet burned. I should have been more careful. I was too confident, and now this.

My friends had walked ahead of me. They didn't hear this silent abduction. The perpetrator dragged me back into a dark doorway. I couldn't fight it. I felt the space between my brows tighten and I couldn't catch a rhythm in my breath. My chest was tight. He turned me around and let go of my mouth. He growled into my ear, "I'm going to remove my hand from your mouth. You're a smart girl. You won't make a sound."

It was Jadel! I nodded.

He was wrapped inside a hooded black uniform like a ninja. It didn't make me feel any better that it was him because his motivation was so obviously twisted. Those mesmerizing eyes were something else to me now. They were being used for the highest form of trickery and this time I was far from enticed.

"You should have listened to me," he snarled.

My eyes shot off daggers at him— was he insane?! He says he knows I'm smart but then he suggests I should have made a stupid choice. "Listen to *you*!?"

"Look what's happening!" His whisper was on fire.

"Jadel, *you* did this! You're S.O.I.L.?!"

"There is no time to talk the politics of our backgrounds. You accept I am with you or you convince yourself I am against you. But despite how you define me, you must know that intelligence is hot onto you. I will protect you—"

"S.O.I.L. has never protected me!"

"Yes, I am clandestino for the society. I have deber civico, but my allegiance is to your father."

"You know my dad?!"

"I told you you were mi amiga. I never lied to you."

I saw truth in his eyes, but I couldn't help but doubt him, too. Was he being honest with me or still blowing smoke to lure me into his web? My devil's advocate was coming on strong and rightfully so.

"How do I know you're telling the truth this time?"

"You don't. When it comes to people there is no absolute truth. Trusting people is always an act of faith. You take information, you follow your instincts. Do what you must and I will do the same. I have an obligation here. Right now that is to contain you, alive and well."

"They can't ever contain me."

"Oh but they can. The reason you are here and still alive is because that is what they want."

"But why?!"

"There is one person on earth that can influence your father. Do you know who that is?"

It had to be me. But I was perplexed. I had no idea what they expected I would achieve for them, and they were terribly mistaken if they believed I would just be some sheep in their herd.

"I am going to find my dad, and they can't stop me."

"From your mouth to God's ears. But you need to be aware of the impact it will have if you're caught."

"I think I know what they're capable of."

"I see. You think it's been bad so far? Wrong. I've seen what they can do, and they've gone easy on you."

I gulped. It felt like I was on the verge of being zapped into a gas but also incredibly close to reconnecting with my father who would never let anyone harm me. "I'll take my chances."

"I know you will, and I will do my best to protect you, but you've made it extremely difficult."

I saw movement out of the corner of my eye. Jadel's head snapped to look quicker than I could, but within a second we both had eyes on Dom, who froze in his tracks, assessing the situation.

Jadel whispered to me, "You cannot tell a soul we had this conversation or it puts everything with your father in great danger."

Dom suddenly sprinted in our direction. Jadel pushed me out towards Dom and I stumbled to the ground, taking my fall with the palms of my hands.

"Doro!" Dom screamed as he reached me. "You alright?"

We both looked up. Jadel was gone.

"We can't be out here like this!" I exclaimed as I pushed myself up.

"I got you—"

Dom helped me up and put my arm around his shoulder.

18

MY FRIENDS AND I agreed that the most cautious way to proceed was for Dom and I to stay back in a hiding spot while they went out to determine the exact whereabouts of my dad. They had a whole lot working in their favor: safety in numbers, Intuerian instincts, Giancarlo's knowledge of the language and geography of this hub, and Anika's wisdom. I had confidence in them.

This nook Dom and I were in was one of those rare places in Seneca that did not pick up any signal. I did a good job of quickly selecting the people inside this secret society that knew where these types of places were, like Giancarlo. Dom and I sat in a stairwell between two connected levels where experiments being conducted with the blue liquid were taking place. It was dark in the nook, but we had the indirect blue glow giving us just enough cool illumination to see each other.

The second that Anika, Reba and Giancarlo cleared the area, Dom got right to it. "What was that all about?"

"You saw. I almost got caught by S.O.I.L. It was such a relief you showed up when you did."

Dom took a beat, and in that silence I died just a little. My gaze on him broke. My eyes hit the ground, my feet— of course they started to overheat. I'm sure this behavior was telling. I just didn't know what to say. Dom did—

"I was watching you for longer than you saw me standing there."

Oh no.

"Okay," I meekly replied.

"Want to tell me anything?"

I did. I so did. This was the worst. "There is so much I want to tell you."

He was at the edge of his patience and the trust between us was on the line once again, but I was stuck. Jadel warned me that telling anyone could put everything with my dad in danger, but I needed to share everything with Dom from now on. Even so, I hesitated.

"So tell me, Doro." There was urgency in his voice. I knew this conversation could make or break us.

I reached for his hand. He pulled it away. This was the body language of a guy protecting himself from me. I hated this position. I was close to him and alone with him but completely disconnected from him. As the silence grew so did the distance between us. I opened my mouth but couldn't make words come out. If I didn't tell him, he would hate me. We had just started the rekindling process. Honesty was essential to our survival. But if I did tell him, I could compromise the security for each of us and create a terrible domino effect that I could not reverse.

"I figured this is how it would be," he said. His piercing stare killed me.

"Dom."

"Doro, something is going on. I could tell you knew that guy."

He looked to me for anything. I nodded slightly. Baby steps.

"I just don't get why it's so hard for you to be forthcoming."

"It's not—"

"Then who is he?"

I searched Dom's face for any trace of mercy for me on this one, but all I saw was rising angst. All this time I'd been so hung up on how destroyed I had been in missing him, but it was clear here that I was the destroyer, and I couldn't stop it.

"Why are you protecting that guy?" He couldn't make sense of it and I couldn't explain it.

"I'm not protecting him, I'm protecting *you* and our friends. If I say anything about that situation, I could be jeopardizing everything. Is that what you want?"

"I just want the truth."

"Sometimes it's not that easy."

"Your M.O. It's just too hard to be honest."

"This doesn't have anything to do with honesty."

"It does. I wish you could just tell me who he is and what that was about. I don't care if it is dangerous information. What's dangerous is being in love with a girl who feels like she can't tell me anything."

I imploded. While my body was inside out, I begged my heart for the answer to this one. What I came out with was—

"His name is Jadel. He found me on the verge of death, he helped me regain my energy and he brought me into Hub 48 through a secret passageway."

Dom sat back. The truth wasn't comfortable. We'd already established that.

"Dom?"

"What else?"

"Not much, other than the fact that, once we were in, I realized he was S.O.I.L., and everything changed."

"Jeez, Doro. What changed? Did you have feelings for him?"

"Feelings like?"

Dom raised his shaking voice, "Feelings, Doro."

"Dom stop. Look, I'm being honest with you, you can't freak out."

Dom bit the inside of his lip. I could tell he was trying to cool it and just listen, but he had to know everything. "What happened to you out in the woods? What happened in those twenty seven days. Were you with him? Is that why you cut me off on FigureFlex?"

"What? No. Dom, you know I was hacked and he was a

helping hand."

"He was manipulating you!"

"Maybe, but he kept me alive. And I was using him too."

"Oh my god, Doro."

"Dom. Don't start taking this off in every direction. There is only one objective here."

"I know that."

"You wanted the truth and this is it."

"You're right, but you *gotta* know we can't trust him."

"We won't." I could tell that made Dom feel a little better as he unscrunched his lips and relaxed his shoulders.

"I wish I could say something to make everything right, but I am fending off delirium here."

Dom gently reached for my head and pulled it to his chest.

"You don't have to say anything else."

We lay back against the wall. The tensions we had subsided as we allowed ourselves the moment to just be.

19

THE INTEL THAT Reba, Anika and Giancarlo uncovered indicated that my dad was probably in the main vessel where the highest level of classified Doromium applications took place. So, along with those three and Dom, I took a clear ascension dome down through layers upon layers of earth. We passed millions of years of rock formations and sedimentary deposits as we descended through the Crust of the Earth into the Upper Mantle. As we glided down this cool, gray, grainy chute, it was wild to envision the digging that took place to penetrate this amount of granite. This was the deepest I'd been inside Seneca, in more ways than one.

Inside the Dm sector there were various elevators to different vessels, each containing Doromium experiments of their own, but our ascension dome didn't stop. The findings of my dad's mind were literally the driving force behind all of these incredible studies, which was nuts, considering he discovered it from scratch. Even though I didn't know exactly what

Doromium was and what it could do, I wasn't surprised that it was something pretty darn phenomenal. I couldn't wait to find out.

Our ride down came to a stop and the door opened to a one-hundred-percent dark gray stone room the size of a few closets. We didn't waste a second before we stepped off and flex-entered through a stone doorway into an enormous underground system. On the other side of a clear glass wall, a river of blue flowed up a giant glass tube into an orb the size of a mansion where gasses were bubbling and brewing. Monitors conducting data encircled the tube with scientists analyzing and comparing notes. This operation dwarfed Operation Crystal by any measure. I took in its grandiosity. We all did. Something incredibly life changing was going on here.

I lowered my eyes from the gaseous ball to land on the profile of a man standing behind a screen that was like the one Anika had in her secret medical chamber, only it was ten times the size. The man was orchestrating equations on the screen, before a panel of scientists. I felt my bones tingle before it registered in my mind: The man was my dad.

My dad stopped orchestrating. He was twenty yards away from me, tops. He paused and then he turned his head. His big sky blue eyes landed right on me and it was as if he'd seen a ghost. I swear the color in his already pale face vanished and his eyes glazed over. He placed his hand up to the top of his chest near his neck. He tilted his head ever so slightly to the right like he always did when analyzing something that wasn't mathematical. It was a shot of nostalgia straight to my heart.

"Daddy," I muttered under my breath, like I was a little girl again. The last time I saw him I was just barely a teenager, and now, I was practically an adult.

My friends didn't say a word. They all looked in through the glass, and then back at me, in total silence, respecting the fact that this was no small moment. I tried to speak and the sound that came out of my mouth sounded like gibberish, "Aghoostoblichash— blughblugh— ohhwhumm." Horrified, I looked to Anika and frantically shook my head. Then, I quickly looked back at my dad. I didn't want him to disappear from my sight.

Dom stepped in to hold my arm. "What's happening to her?!"

Anika maintained her calm. "I'm not surprised. Your speech has been intercepted."

"They're relentless," Dom added.

I stared at my dad. He rubbed his hand along his jawbone, staring back at me, processing a moment that probably hit him like a ton of bricks. I plastered my hand on the glass. He started towards me from the other side and the scientists behind him looked on, intrigued and confused.

Anika grasped my head with her hands and turned me to face her, scanning my eyes with her red-framed flexer glasses. When she let go, I flung my gaze back to my dad walking towards me.

Anika spoke up louder than her normal calm self, "Just what I suspected. You've got a hardware visitor in there that's overriding the master in your flex implant to block the language center of your brain."

"Christ!" Dom shouted.

"Keep your cool, Dominic."

"This isn't looking good, you guys," Reba added with a shaky voice.

I tried to speak again. "Meeuulipp-aaahhraa!" My frustrations flared. My dad was only several feet away from me, but on the other side of an incredibly thick clear wall. I could see him, but I couldn't reach him. I was on the verge of hyperventilation. I felt it climbing up my legs...

Dom took my hand. "Don't panic, we'll figure this out."

Anika launched a screen in front of herself. "I'll see if I can get a read on the signals that your flexer picks up so we can understand the blocks going into your brain."

My long-awaited reunion with my dad was burdened by interference and obstacles. He reached the glass and his eyes searched my face, looking for his little girl. But there wasn't a little girl here anymore. I could see his inner dialogue just by looking into his eyes. Mine were the same as his, just a different color. It was clear he knew there was a heavy backstory just in the fact that I was standing before him, and he could also decipher that his little girl was being manipulated. My dad was no fool.

His lips mouthed, "I'm sorry." Even though I heard not a sound, his words hit me hard. I heard them in his arms hanging at his side with his shoulders rounded forward and his palms facing me, his clenched brows and quivering lips. Face-to-face with my dad, his nerves washed over me. He looked helpless, apologetic, but also overcome with joy to see me.

The echo of my heartbeat was the only intelligible sound my body could produce while a bucket of words filled up at the top of my throat, unable to come out.

Booming alarms suddenly pierced the quiet and the lights went out. I threw my hands to my ears. My friends all covered theirs, too. I looked through to my dad; his side of the glass was still lit up. He started yelling, and his colleagues began to scramble for help. I'd never seen my dad so intense. Blood filled the whites of his eyes. There was no sound, but the veins bulging in his neck and forehead were loud enough. This whole time I couldn't hear him, but I understood him completely.

Then the lights went out completely. My dad was gone.

20

I WAS BEING transported upwards at an alarmingly high speed. Nothing was touching my body yet I couldn't move. My eyes weren't covered with a blindfold or anything, but I couldn't see a thing. Just black. I blinked, hoping for something to appear, even those annoying little flashes you see after a light shines in your eye. Anything, literally *anything* would be good to see. But there was nothing. My heart pounded out of control and my throat started to close as I imagined this could be permanent: blind and mute forever. My ultimate punishment for defying the law and order of S.O.I.L. But I didn't even know for sure that it was S.O.I.L. that had me. I just knew that *someone* had me. Someone that didn't like that I'd found my dad.

Some forces out there were intentionally keeping me and my dad apart. I would not rest until I found out exactly who they were and why they didn't want us to reunite. I had failed at reaching my dad and I couldn't be mad at anyone but myself for being so naive to the dangers of the flex implant and for thinking

I could outsmart anyone who got into my flexer. But it didn't matter. It didn't matter. "What's done is done…" they say, and now I was just scared.

I tried to keep calm but my heart had a different plan. It pounded like a deep bass drum in a hollow cave. Every sound reverberated. A pressure built up between my eyes and extended up to my forehead and down between my ears.

Was this also happening to the others? I could neither see nor hear them.

We stopped.

I recognized the gentle swoosh of an acoustic carrier door opening. I was moved into it by a set of large hands that suddenly gripped my upper arms. I flinched and we were off.

We traveled about three minutes before we came to a stop. The hands pushed at my back, urging me to walk again. I did. Until I could see, hear and speak again I was going to do exactly what was requested of me. Well, maybe not *exactly* everything but I was going to choose my battles to the best of my mentally-compromised ability.

This walk only lasted a few moments and then I was brought to a stop, and moved into a seat.

I suddenly got a cranial flex. *Doro?! Are you getting this?*

Dom!

Dom, help me, I can't see anything! I flexed back at lightning speed, not knowing if my flexes could be sent off because I couldn't speak and I wasn't sure if this attack on me affected words from coming out of me altogether, even in thought form. But I tried anyways.

Try not to freak out, I'm your eyes for now. They've got us all in a room. You, me, Anika, Giancarlo and Reba.

Okay, it worked! I could send and receive encrypted messages through cranial flexes, but I couldn't speak my thoughts. Thank goodness Dom had that flex implant too so that we could communicate virtually in these crucial moments.

Who? Who is here?! I flexed Dom.

Dom fired back: *Three men in black— S.O.I.L., I'm sure. And now someone else is coming into the room.*

I can't see or speak! What is happening to me?!

I have no idea. But we're going to fix this, we're working on it —

Work fast, Dom, please work fast! Claustrophobia was setting in like I had been buried alive inside a wood coffin.

Dom didn't reply and that didn't make this any easier.

I was there for a long time, as the sound of my speeding heartbeat clashed with the sounds of a muffled debate between several men and a woman. It was literally like I was buried below layers of sand and mud and Dom was above me furiously digging.

What is happening, Dom?

Dom?

Dom!?

21

A SCANNER MOVED across my eyes. It was familiar. Before I had the chance to move, I knew I shouldn't. I was back in a BioNan. I would never forget my first and last time, in Anika's secret chamber of techno-medicine at her ranch in Virginia. Everything was a blur in my brain. But then I saw the light— literally! I started to try and put together what was happening but no sooner than that I was being ejected from this beautiful machine.

As my body made its way out, I looked up to see Anika. I was so glad it was her, and beyond relieved that I could see again.

I immediately got a flex from Dom— *Don't move.* It said.

I didn't. I could see in my periphery that I was on a portable BioNan island in a large, dull metallic gold room. My mind was emerging from a muggy fog, but I was perfectly aware of everything that had happened to me leading up to this point.

Dom had extreme efficiency with his flex delivery. *Giancarlo got us in here by convincing the higher-ups that you were in grave danger with your implant and if they didn't oblige, you could die and their lives would be on the line.*

None of this was making sense. I needed to get my mind and body back stat. *I don't understand.*

They know you're John Campbell's daughter, Doro. And John Campbell, as you guessed, is really important around here. If anything happens to you while you're under their watch, they're as good as dead to Seneca.

This was insane. I mean, one octillion percent beyond insane. *Why am I in a BioNan?*

Anika wiped your operating system and rebooted to purge the malware that was messing you up.

I furrowed my brow, feeling slightly violated even though I realized it needed to happen. No sooner than I had the thought, Dom flexed me again.

We had no choice, you were completely under siege.

He was correct, and I did feel quite relieved, however— *Something doesn't feel right, Dom.*

I know. This is obviously way more complex than a simple reboot, and Anika will talk to you about that, but we right now we just need to get out of here—

How?

The guys and I are going to rush them, you and Anika run.

I looked around and realized Dom, Reba and Giancarlo were sitting at a long rectangular table right behind me. Three S.O.I.L. men in black were directly behind them. I could sense that something was about to happen. Reba looked terrified, Giancarlo was blank. I knew this wasn't right. I had to act fast.

Dom, it won't work, you won't be able to get the door open.

I'll steal their flexers, I'll make it happen.

Flexers. Flexers! That was it. The three men in black all had Flexer watches. I had to get into them.

Don't do it. I flexed Dom quick.

We have no other choice! We have to get out before we meet our next fate.

Sit tight. I replied.

I looked to the flexers on the men in black. Dom saw where I was looking and understood where I was going with this. We gave each other a knowing look. He nudged Reba. Reba already knew. He nodded at me.

I powered up my FlexOculi and ran my sensor to pick up the signals from the three flexers belonging to the men in black. It gave me a rush that my system was back in order and I was jumping right back into my groove. I ran some coding and broke into their most basic functions. I scrolled cranially to their flexer command centers, to the morph command, and activated liquid handcuffs.

I shifted my attention back to the three men as their watches turned to handcuffs. Bingo!

They started yelling in Spanish and tried to get control of their flexers but they couldn't. The control was all mine now.

Back to my FlexOculi. I commanded the cuffs to slowly tighten.

The men started shouting as the cuffs squeezed their wrists. They dropped to their knees, no longer shouting but squealing in pain and trying to break free from the cuffs.

I stood up. "Open the door," I ordered.

"Never!" One of the men screamed through spit and gritted teeth.

I remained calm, looked to my friends and nodded— they all stood by my side. I went back to my FlexOculi and commanded the cuffs to tighten more. I looked back to the men on the ground. One of them threw his arms in the air and begged for me to make it stop, but instead I just tightened it a notch more, cutting into skin…

"Command open door or you lose your hands in three… two…"

"Okay! Okay!" The pleading man writhed in pain as the other two were curled over their own hands.

Through a whimper the man commanded, "Open door."

22

LESS THAN A hundred seconds after we had escaped through the door, Dom, Reba, Anika, Giancarlo and I were riding an empty acoustic carrier. Everyone sat dead still with stoic looks, but Dom was anxious. His knee bounced up and down and he just couldn't keep still. I didn't know what the immediate plan was, but along with my friends we would find the way. I had lost faith in me by myself. I'd danced with defeat. But these people lifted me. I put my hand on Dom's bouncing leg. "Try and chill."

Dom stopped moving and looked at me resolutely. "They know Anika is not a Senecan and were prepared to *take care of her*. There is no way I can chill."

I understood. Anika meant the world to Dom and his family.

The acoustic carrier stopped and opened to a twelve-by-twelve version of the safe-deposit room at the bank.

Giancarlo got off first and walked up to a glossy gray panel on the wall. He put his flexer up to it and illuminated buttons instantly appeared, with numbers and symbols like those on a classic keyboard. We stood behind him as he tapped twelve different buttons in the air. The wall with the panel on it then disappeared, leaving us looking out over a massive power grid.

The five of us stepped across a slim metal walkway toward a set of stairs that led down into the field of panels. Not just any field, but like *many* football fields, with a circumference I couldn't determine because my eyes couldn't see that far. It was incredible!

"What is this?" I asked. Ahh, my first words since the brain invasion!

"It's our way out," Giancarlo said.

Dom and I looked at each other puzzled. Dom asked, "What goes on here, Giancarlo? We've never seen a place like this in our hub."

Giancarlo waved us along. "I will tell you about it as we go, but we need to keep moving."

The five of us hurried down the stairs and onto a pathway through the power field. Giancarlo gave us the lowdown as we ran along the sleek cement. "There are five Dynamo Zones in Seneca hubs around the world and each has emergency ascension domes for evacuation to the Aboves."

"What exactly happens in these zones?" Anika asked.

"They are harvesting energy from Earth's core," Giancarlo replied.

"Come again?" I asked, a little short of breath as we ran

between the glossy black, airplane-sized panels that towered over us. I could feel something brewing underneath by way of the warm, vibrating ground.

Giancarlo kept going. "The earth has a molten layer in its outer core and the theory is that in Seneca we transfer the energy that comes from that into power."

Impressive. Earth's resources were being used on a whole new level here. I hated Seneca, but, man, did I love Seneca.

Reba didn't look too surprised, so I had to ask, "Did you know about this?"

Out of breath and sweating like crazy, he nodded.

I stopped in my tracks but kept moving all in the same stride, "I can't believe you knew about this and never said anything."

"I have a certain type of clearance, Campbella."

I scoffed. But then again, I bet my dad would say the same thing. I had to learn to not be mad at my loved ones for their obligatorily clandestine behavior.

Anika stopped and hunched over. "Can we take a breath?"

Dom helped hold her up. "You alright, Anika?"

She tried to stand and make it look like nothing was wrong, but her skin was clammy and pale. Still, she assured us, "I'm fine."

The two Intuerians didn't give off the vibe that we were fine though, and I fed off of that. Giancarlo motioned for us to keep going. "We can't stop."

Dom's adrenaline was cranking. "I'll carry you," he said to Anika. He bent down for her to climb on to his back, but she was too weak and looked like she was about to pass out. Reba helped hold her up by one of her arms and said, "She's dehydrated and her blood pressure is really low. We need to get her out of here."

I knew that help was not coming from inside this hub considering Anika wasn't even Senecan. Anika was an alien here. She'd probably get thrown in some crazy isolation chamber only to be left for dead. Under no circumstance could we let Anika get caught, but more importantly, I couldn't leave. There were more questions now than there were when I set out to come here. There was a reason for this level of secrecy and attempts to control the flow of information inside Seneca. It was no longer a question as to whether or not my dad was here, but now I couldn't leave before speaking with him, face-to-face. As much as I cared for Anika, I couldn't let my mission end because of this situation.

Reba and I helped her up onto Dom's back. He held tight onto her legs as she hunched over his shoulder. We jogged a hundred yards more to the entrance of the emergency ascension dome as my mind raced through ways to say what needed to be said—that I couldn't go with them.

Anika mustered enough strength to barely open her eyes and look at me and me only. A fluttering inclination told me that this would be the last time we would ever see each other. I remembered having that feeling with my grandmother in her hospital bed, and then she passed a few hours later. My heart was heavy and my mind was running fast. It was almost too much for my body to handle.

"What's going on here is something truly exceptional, and it's up to you to ensure it's on the right trajectory," she whispered to me.

"I will do my best." I meant it. I didn't find my purpose. My purpose found me.

She went on, "It won't be easy. Where there is knowledge, there will always be an evil force out there trying to control it. And that force will stop at nothing because knowledge is power."

Anika suddenly got woozy.

"Anika—" I took her arm. It was crazy to be on the opposite side here. I was used to Anika looking out for me when I was messed up. But right now she was hanging on by a thread. "Don't worry, you're almost out of here. The guys will make sure you are okay. I am grateful for you, Anika. I never would have made it this far if it wasn't for you."

Anika smiled as her head swayed. Dom's mind was set on getting her to safety, "Let's do this!"

Reba, Giancarlo, Dom and Anika boarded the carrier. My feet stayed planted right where they were. I recalled what Jadel said to me when I first met him and it all made sense to me now. *"Worry is an illusion and what will be, will be."* I knew I couldn't stop seeking answers and knowledge because problems might arise.

They all looked back at me, discovering one by one that I wasn't coming along. Dom looked at me with big ol' Basset Hound eyes and a shaky bottom lip. He bit it to stop the quiver. He shook his head "no" ever-so-slightly. I nodded "yes" just a little bit more. It was, 'I'm sorry, I have to' without actually saying the words. I knew that my staying was exactly what I needed to do. This wasn't about worrying what might happen if S.O.I.L. were to catch me or if Anika didn't make it. Nobody ever said the truth was easy, but no matter how hard it was to find, that is what I was going to do.

Dom's instinct to protect me was overriding our shared goal to save the world. "I can't leave you here," he insisted.

I had to let down his big heart without breaking it. I hoped he would understand, but I knew I couldn't let the worry mess me up.

"This is not you leaving me. This is us making sure our friends make it out and we succeed. My mind is clear now, thanks to you guys, and I know what I need to do. What *we* need to do. You need to get Anika to safety and make it back to our hub with Reba."

Everyone had sacrifices to make and everyone knew it. Dom also knew that once my mind was set, there was no changing it. He was drowning in worry, and for now, for us, distance was the only way.

"I love you," I said, believing in my heart that this wasn't it for us.

He reached for my hand and kissed it.

"I love you," he replied. Now I had a stockpile of ammunition.

Giancarlo held his flexer to the control panel. "This is it."

Dom and I were locked on each other.

"Come back, Doro," he said.

"She will," Reba said.

The door closed.

23

I BELIEVED GIANCARLO knew his way in and out and that Dom and Reba would get Anika to safety. Unfortunately, that couldn't be my concern. The entirety of my focus had to be on reuniting with my dad and bringing down the house.

With every breath I took inside Seneca, I inhaled more and more of an understanding of its capacity to heal the world. I knew it all along, but the kicker was, as my understanding grew, so did my responsibility to make things right. The corruption inside Seneca needed to be exposed. Nobody should have cancer. We have the cure, yet people are still dying from it. That injustice wasn't gonna fly as long as my heart was beating.

I made my way through this hub by means of piggybacked flex recognition data that I had snatched off the random scientist from S.I.C.E. Regardless, I still needed to watch my back because S.O.I.L. could be one step ahead of me. I was humbled by the realization that my skills were not perfect and that there were others out there that could do what I could do, even bigger, better and faster.

S.I.C.E. was on lockdown. I received a flex alert that was sent to the person I was piggybacking:

"Citizens: There has been a security breach inside S.I.C.E., and access has been shut down until further notice. You will be able to exit and travel to your residences. S.O.I.L. advises and expects you to report suspicious behaviors."

Since I was in S.I.C.E. and, last I knew, my dad was, too, I couldn't leave and expect to get back in without a fight. Instead, my intention was to lay low and let them believe that my friends and I were no longer inside this hub.

With my head down and eyes up I stepped off the acoustic carrier back into an area not too far from where we were just being held. There was no way they would think I would come back to the very place from which I had just escaped. I'd say I did a pretty excellent job of staying in the shadows and scanning my surroundings for potential threats.

I turned into a hallway that led to the exact spot where I had seen my dad. It was pretty empty and I was surprised. Where had everyone gone? I doubted that my dad would be here after what had happened, but it was only a matter of time until he returned.

A few people passed by quickly and I could tell there was an edge in the air. So I stopped a woman in a lab coat. "Excuse me, is something wrong?" She was caught off guard and it didn't seem like she wanted to stay and chat, at all. Not because of me, but because of the current situation.

"Mi English not so good."

So I asked again in Spanish and she was quick to answer warmly, but with a warning in her voice. She explained that a while back they had experienced a security breach in S.I.C.E. that had harmed a lot of people. I didn't quite understand how what I was doing could affect anyone on that level, but I started to feel guilty. It was possible that, because I hadn't calculated all the possible outcomes of my actions, I had put hundreds, if not thousands of people in danger. It killed me that they had accepted the opportunity to experience life 2.0 just like me, and I infringed upon that for them in some way.

The woman pushed a smile through her otherwise stoic face, wished me a good afternoon and briskly continued on. It seemed like the last few people in this hallway wanted to get the heck out, so my instinct told me to follow suit.

It was only a matter of milliseconds before I found out why. I had just a hundred yards to go before reaching the next entryway I needed to take, but I only made it a half of another step before the single most piercing sound in the history of sounds rippled through my ear drums and sizzled my brain! My eyes rolled back in my head as I slumped down into a pile on the floor, squeezing at my head. What in the world was happening?!

My vision was bombarded with flashes of white and I couldn't see a thing beyond the tip of my nose. My body crumbled to the ground and I contorted into the fetal position. I lost all control of my body!

Within seconds I was swiftly scooped up and moved down the hall, and I actually breathed a sigh of relief. I was incapacitated but something was happening and anything was better than being idle. I didn't care who had me because I'd rather die than be in this state much longer— one hundred percent immobilized but still cognizant of all that was happening. What a horrifying feeling! I'd seen a bunch of TV shows from the olden days where people had to overcome crazy, physically trying obstacles and eat weird foods and I would think to myself, "I could never do that." Well, the past nine months of my life had been nothing but that and here I was doing it. My life was shaping out to be a testament to the adage, "What doesn't kill you makes you stronger." In this moment of being completely incapable of moving I felt myself gaining strength.

I was pushed through an arched doorway into another hallway. My senses were fully restored, the piercing sound was gone and I could feel my arms, legs, fingers… I looked down to see cuffs on my hands and ankles. I was being briskly rolled along by two individuals in all black with gray robotic headpieces. Those helmets most likely provided them with immunity to whatever in the world just crippled me back there. Actually, could it be those helmets that created a sensory attack on me?

I had to get my hands on one of those helmets.

I wanted to flex Dom but I knew I couldn't because he would most definitely come back for me. I had to ride this out on my own for so many reasons. Mainly to keep them safe and separate from me.

24

THE TWO GUYS in helmets maneuvered me on wheels down an empty, flat-grey hall that took a number of sharp turns. With several quick blinks my eyes adjusted and regained vision in the dim light. I started to feel the sensation in my body come back but I wasn't about to use any sudden motion on these two.

We reached a dead end and an arched doorway opened. I looked inside a room that was strikingly similar to the one in which I had met Frank Wallingsford. A mahogany table sat smack dab in the center, encircled by plush black chairs big enough for elephants. The entire back wall of the room was made of glass, overlooking the most stunning indoor garden that was exploding with spring color from vibrant yellow and orange poppy flowers. Bumblebees and butterflies emerged from flowers to hover when a light mist was turned on. I didn't know if they were real or automated.

Two men in all black stood next to a long table.

No words were spoken as my escorts turned and left, and that felt pretty ominous.

One of the two men in the room motioned for me to take a seat. "Please," he said.

I was perplexed by the pleasantry. I noticed my body was completely back to normal as though nothing had ever happened.

I sat and the man flex-commanded my cuffs to melt away. They turned to water and self-evaporated.

"Señorita Campbell," he said, all long and drawn out and dramatic, "we are sorry this meeting isn't happening under happier circumstances, but we welcome you."

"Gracias," I said, feeling awfully uneasy about this completely unpredictable state of flux. Was this some new interrogation tactic they were trying out? I knew how S.O.I.L. felt about me, and playing nice had never been one of their tactics. Not that this was one hundred percent S.O.I.L., but let's be real.

"What you just experienced is an ultrasonic sensory disrupter that renders you incapable of doing anything physically."

"I noticed."

"We apologize for the inconvenience. We have some guests that will join you," the man said, and then he turned and began to walk out of the room. He stopped before he was out the door to look me dead in the eye. "We just want you to know that it is our priority to ensure your safety."

Yeah right. I feigned the heck out of believing what he was saying.

Both of the men left the room, with me in it, alone, not cuffed. I looked around as if there was a chance I could figure something out and break free, but who was I kidding? Definitely not myself.

Before I dove into another direction of thought, a FigureFlex appeared in the room. Ellen Malone was here. No introduction, no warning, and not surprising at all. She was in one of her suits — gray and white. Ellen looked at me like we were all good and I should have been relieved to see her. I was majorly in the dark and she was clearly in an insightful enough position to be playing both sides of the fence. So I wasn't relieved. I felt quite the opposite.

Ellen Malone knew too much. She knew what I needed to know. Otherwise, why would she be here? I'd played my cards close to the vest all along when it came to Ellen and I was still in the dark, so I decided the better move might be to show some of my cards and maybe she'd show me some of hers.

"You don't seem terribly happy to see me," she said.

"I'm... relieved."

"Relieved? Could have fooled me."

"Are you kidding? Of course I am! I'm in this foreign hub, captured and brought here. It could have been *anyone* that appeared in this room. It could have been someone who wanted me dead, but it's you. Shouldn't I be relieved?"

"If only this was all black and white."

I tilted my head at the burning question and threw one back at her.

"Did you know my dad was here?"

"I think you know at this point that I can't talk about everything I know, Doro."

"This isn't just plain old everything, this is my dad!"

"I understand why you're emotional. Just know that if I can't talk about a person, place or thing, it means it very likely has a considerable significance to Seneca."

She did know.

The doorway opened and another man walked in. The room seemed to get smaller and my breath became audibly tarnished with worry. This new guy was an unassuming dad type with a butt chin and dimples. Charming off the bat. He smiled from his eyes. "Buenos dias."

I looked to Ellen to see if she knew him.

"Doro, this is Senator Gilroy."

Wow... now *this* was interesting.

"It's very nice to meet you, Dorothy."

Very interesting. "Nice to meet you," I replied.

"I understand you're friendly with my daughter."

"Yeah— yes." Although I didn't want to implicate Brittany in any of this, I did want to stay on the up and up in the moment.

"She speaks highly of you."

Okay. I was just going to keep my speaking to an absolute

minimum because I had absolutely no idea what Brittany had or hadn't said to her dad.

He continued, "I know this must seem strange and you're probably unsure of our intentions, so we'll just skip the politics and lay it out as straightforward as possible. How does that sound?"

"Is that really an option?"

He laughed. It was genuine. "It really is," he answered. "First of all, Doro, you need to know that we made the choice for you to come to Seneca in the first place and we *wanted* you to see your dad. We're pretty darn impressed with how quickly you made that happen."

A nervous little laugh escaped me. "What?" I asked. No way. These people were all looking at me like they knew everything and I was just this pitiful heap of teenager. "You really think I would believe that?" I quipped.

"Why not?" Senator Gilroy asked.

"Do you have any idea what I went through to get here?"

"Actually, yes," Gilroy responded with sheer confidence.

Ellen quickly chimed in as she so often does, "Doro, we know all of it. And even though you don't know the magnitude of what you're involved with, you do know that it is something massive. Otherwise why would you risk everything to get the implant, take Brittany's recognition data to get here, and make the choice to eat that river snail?"

"You know about the snail? Then you knew I was out there and what was happening to me and you didn't do anything to help me?!"

"Sometimes *help* doesn't come in the most warm and fuzzy forms."

"Forget warm and fuzzy. I almost died, Ellen!"

Senator Gilroy swooped in to her defense, "Why do you think Ellen came for you in the first place?" He was remarkably calm and focused. But I wasn't. My feet were hot and my stomach was tied in a rope knot. I needed to steady myself, untie the knot and absorb the issue at hand. I stared Ellen down and succumbed to the realization that, in actuality, I didn't have an answer. *Why did she actually bring me to Seneca?*

"I can't imagine that at this point you'd really think I brought you here simply because you're great at math," Ellen said.

Why hadn't I analyzed all of this more thoroughly before? I was pissed at myself, pissed at her and I couldn't begin to know what I should say or do next. Actually, scratch that, I did know. "From this point forward I say nothing and I do nothing until I get a meeting with my dad."

Gilroy didn't miss a beat. "Your father is currently being briefed on your history with Seneca."

My eyes widened, then shifted to the ground. Gilroy kept talking but it didn't register because my brain and FlexOculi had just sprung into action, flinging out images that mapped a visual timeline across the floor: Ellen Malone in my room, getting the Necrolla Carne vaccine at Claytor Lake, meeting Dom in S.E.R.C., everything the two of us went through with the nanobots, the mosquitoes, the drones, S.O.I.L. chasing us on the Brooklyn Bridge, the trial in the salt mine, the Peruvian wilderness, the brain invasion— jeez. I wondered what parts my dad would be made privy to and what they would leave out.

No matter how hard Ellen and Senator Gilroy tried to sell me on their allegiance to me and my dad, I could not be convinced. It would have to take words straight out of my dad's mouth and into my ears for me to believe.

In walked Jadel. All that time I'd spent with a guy who seemed so genuine and sweet and I still didn't know him at all. I literally had no clue who this guy really was or to whom he owed his allegiance. Our relationship was an illusion as far as I was concerned.

FigureFlex Ellen looked to me. "Doro, you know Jadel."

Why didn't she just hit me in the head with a bat? I nodded.

"More than *knows*!" he exclaimed.

I scoffed. It was a natural reflex.

"Jadel is going to escort you to your dad."

"Of course he is, and I'm sure I should also believe he was planning on escorting me to my dad this whole time."

"Actually, yes," Ellen said, quite confidently.

"Unbelievable."

I crossed my arms and looked away from them.

Jadel put his hand on my shoulder, "Doro don't be mad. I protected you, I got you inside Seneca just as you wished and—"

"But you're with S.O.I.L.," I snarled, and pushed his hand off my shoulder.

"And?" He totally didn't get why that was a problem. "So what?"

Ellen interjected, "Doro, you should probably take a moment before we discuss this any further. Pause and play out your options in your head."

I had *already* played it out, and my options were pretty clear. Either resist the path they were trying to send me on, and see how that would go, or follow along. The reality was that if they wanted me dead, I would already be six-feet-under… and I was way further down than that. I wasn't agreeing to a thing until I spoke to my father.

25

SHORTLY AFTER CONTEMPLATING depths, I found myself descending into the earth in a small gray dome. I swept the tip of my tongue against the back of my grimy teeth. I was ravenous and knew I wouldn't be eating any time soon. As the thought swept my mind, my stomach gurgled long and deep. Any energy I had came from the steady stream of adrenaline that ran through me.

I held my focus on the ground directly in front of my feet as Jadel's deep green eyes burned a hole in me. Apparently he didn't need a queue to attempt a dialogue. This guy was subtly bold. "We are on the same team, Doro," he said.

Here we go. I didn't acknowledge him.

Jadel continued, "I was just doing my job. Find you and guide you."

Okay, I had to call B.S. "Straight into the enemy's arms?!"

"Not at all. We agreed that you would stay where I left you until I returned. You didn't. Some of that chaos could have been avoided if you had just waited."

"Waited for what? To get captured because you were setting me up?"

"Not at all."

"Good thing I followed you and found out you were with S.O.I.L., before it was too late."

"It's true that I was assigned to your detail by S.O.I.L., but S.O.I.L. isn't just bad."

Jadel and I stared each other down. I feigned indifference, but that didn't stump him. He spoke with passion, "I left you so that I could tell them you escaped at the train after I found you. That was to divert their search for you to far away from here. I was going to come back and bring you to your dad."

"Why would you do such a thing?"

"I already explained this to you. My allegiance is to your father and the protection of Doromium. Period."

Jadel lifted his Dm pendant.

Wow. The Dm stood for *Doromium*— that emblem was all over Seneca. My outdated defense mechanisms screamed, "Don't fall for it!" But this totally added up. Jadel wasn't playing games. In fact, in thinking back, he hadn't told one lie that I knew of.

Our vessel stopped. A door opened with a quiet swoosh and my face was lit by that seductive, glowing blue hue. I looked to Jadel. With his hand he requested I step off. I did because I wanted to, not because he asked me to.

Behind him, I saw the outline of a man's shoulder in the light. It was a stance I knew like the back of my hand. I took a few more steps in and the man took a few steps towards me, too, so that we were both under the same light. My eyes fell to my dad's and I froze. So did he. In an absolute beat of disbelief my heart fluttered and grabbed for this moment to stick. It felt like a dream, but it wasn't. Surreal began to hand the reins over to real. My dad and I were breathing the same air. The vast space between us shrunk to nothing as he hugged me. Love and comfort filled me up. I held on. For the first time in a long time I held onto someone and I could not let go. I just couldn't. He held on to me just as hard. I don't think I took a breath in those moments, but, when I finally did, it was a deep, eyes-closed, massive, stretched-to-the limits inhale. I held it all in at the top of my lungs and exhaled all the toxic crap.

"Dad." I was hurt but bursting with happiness to be with him. He wasn't a hologram. He wasn't a memory.

"Doro," he said, as I took my first breath back in.

"You're alive," I whispered back, "I knew it."

My dad nodded. "Of course I am."

It was the truest thing I'd said since he'd been gone. My heart was realizing a relief it had been seeking for years, through a thousand cries, and a million breaths. It was a relief that spread through my whole being and washed away all the scars of foul play. But I was so hurt by him, knowing he let us believe he was as good as dead.

My dad's breaths were short and hard and they made me worry. He looked like he was in extreme emotional turmoil and he didn't know how to release any of it. I had my music as an escape, and he used to have his long walks outdoors— but this was far from the great outdoors. He didn't talk. He just stared at me. "Dad?"

Tears welled up in his eyes. His face was flushed with guilt and happiness and sadness all at the same time. It was like he had so much to say but couldn't find the words. He was never a verbal or outwardly emotional guy. He gently shook his head, I could see the tension in his forehead.

"You chose to leave us?" I asked, scared of his reply.

"I didn't make a choice to leave you."

"Then why?"

"It's not something I can easily explain, and I regret that, even if I try, it won't make sense."

"I've grown up a lot since you saw me last. I can handle the truth."

"Believe me, I have imagined this day over and over again but I just never figured out how this conversation would go. This isn't numbers. It doesn't make sense because there are no correct answers."

My dad fidgeted. He was so great at being in the zone and

solving problems, but when it came to real life emotions and relationships he just kind of froze up. My mom was always so good at getting us to open up and talk in our house. But she wasn't here now and I realized it was up to me.

"Then let's figure it out, together."

My dad smiled. "I'd love that."

"But you have to tell me what is going on. All of it."

My dad gently shook his head. "Where do I even begin?"

"Did they bring you here against your will?" I asked.

"No. I originally came to Seneca because I knew what this meant for the future. It had to happen, Doro. It wasn't a choice."

There it was. I dropped my head. He had chosen Seneca over me.

"Doro, I know it seems like I left you, but you have to believe I never would. I *never* would. It's not all black and white."

"You did leave us, though, and I know it isn't all black and white because in the past four years that you've been gone, I learned the hard way."

I saw it register in my dad's face the instant he realized my innocence was no longer. He shook the look off his face. "We have a lot of catching up to do, but we have to do it in a fragmented fashion because if you know as much as I think you do, you know it's not safe to carry all information of value in one place and time."

"Okay, but I'm just struggling to understand how you could

pick Seneca over mom and me."

"You two are everything to me."

"It doesn't make sense then! Why would you leave us?"

"Doro, it is the hardest choice I have ever made in my life. Stay home and watch the world fall to pieces, or leave everyone I love behind and come here in order to... for lack of less clichéd words, make a better world for you. I say that because I mean it in a perfectly literal sense."

Considering I had been given practically the same ultimatum, I began to empathize with him, and understand how this could have possibly gone down. But I didn't leave my kid. He did.

He continued, "They called us the selfie-generation. Accused us of being self-absorbed and not connected to others. But we didn't create Seneca for ourselves, we created it *for* others. For our children and grandchildren and all the generations to come. I am here because this is it. *This* is my purpose, to do this for you. To leave you the best Earth I can."

We both sat in the space of letting that sink in.

"Why didn't you bring us with you?" I quietly asked.

He hugged me.

"Your life was beautiful when I left. I wasn't going to rip my wife and child away from the life we had, a real life with dirt, sun and ocean, into a social and science experiment. That's what it was when we began, Doro."

Although it somewhat clicked, I was still upset. I knew there were a lot of moving parts and people that had to make this happen, but why did this have to happen to *us*? Surely he was not the only person out of billions that could fix the devastated planet. That just seemed preposterous. Why couldn't my dad have been selfish? Why couldn't that have been the world I got to live in?

"I would have so much rather remained in a sucky-polluted world with you in it than some cleaned-up leisure world without you," I said.

"Doro, those were never options. I know it doesn't seem like it, but I always planned on coming back for you."

"When?"

"I wish I could tell you what you want to hear. But I can't. I just had to commit to the process of trial and error, by believing that I could succeed and that that time would come."

"It still doesn't make sense."

"I know, but it will. Seneca is not synonymous with instant gratification," my dad replied. "What happens here is the actualization of the thoughts, hopes, and bravery of many more people than me alone. That is what it takes to create a world that can uplift humanity."

"Everyone keeps making blanket statements like that, but you know as well as I do, that means nothing. I need facts. Data. Truth."

"And that is where we go next," he said, finally revealing the confidence in his voice that I once knew. It put me a bit at ease that maybe my dad hadn't simply succumbed to the dream of some unrealistic idyllic world. There was more. There always was... and it was coming.

26

I walked alongside my dad and for those brief moments I felt safe. Normally in these tight, dim tunnels I was claustrophobic, but not this time. Being with my dad gave me an innate sense of security. My cheeks were full with a fruit and nut bar he had given me. Meals were few and far between these days and I got used to surviving in starvation mode.

After zigzagging through a maze that was obviously familiar to my dad, we reached the end of the tunnel. My dad stepped the tips of his tattered sneakers onto a metallic white line on the slate ground and stated his name, "John Campbell, requesting access."

There was a 'swoosh' and a slight wind blew through my hair.

When the door disappeared, a whole other level of incredibleness filled the space before me. It was an enormous expanse illuminated with my beloved soft blue light that emanated from the skyscraper of blue liquid. This area was similar to the place I had first seen my dad on the other side of the glass, only it was the on-steroids version. Cascades of tubes oozing bubbling blue liquid past floor after floor, up and down, for as far as I could see. Dozens of metallic cylinders spread out equidistant. They reached across several hundred yards, with steel walkways and platforms, through which scientists traveled. Propulsion fans the size of the Pacific Wheel on the Santa Monica Pier bookended each side of the expanse.

My dad smiled when he saw the expression on my face— pure awe and wonder. Like a child seeing her first rainbow. My head was frozen in amazement with the rest of my body while my eyes moved about taking it all in.

"This is all for you, Doro. *This* is why I am here. *This* is why we are all here, and *this* is why we will be able to save our planet and stay here. *This*, my love, is the world of Doromium."

Then, none other than Ellen Malone emerged from the blue. Without trepidation, my dad gave her a friendly hug. It didn't sit right in the pit of my stomach. Why was Ellen all over Seneca like she owned the place? Had she been a friend or associate of my dad's all along? She had to be holding something over him. Had she coerced him to come here like she did me? My blood began to boil and this overwhelming protective instinct over my dad kicked in.

Ellen must have noticed the lack of warmth in my eyes. "Doro, I know this seems to just get more and more confusing, but now it will all start to make sense."

"The only thing starting to make sense is that you had a part in taking my dad from us."

"I understand that you're hurt, but please realize nothing I've done has been with a malicious intent. It's actually the opposite."

Meanwhile, the guy I knew who, busy swimming inside his own head, was so often at a loss of words, had just the right words to her defense, "It's true, my love, so much has been at stake. Ellen isn't our enemy. She is a friend and an ally. She dedicated her life to protecting all of this."

I looked at my dad who was both everything to me and a complete stranger. He and Ellen looked at me like I should be happy about this situation. But nothing would make me happy until my family was back together. It was the meddling of outside forces that had destroyed our sweet little peaceful unit to begin with.

Ellen knew my dad was alive this entire time— I imagined from long before she was in my room in Culver City convincing me to come here. She had deceived me and she had deceived my mom. She had literally put my life in danger. I felt sad for my dad that she had managed to pull one over on him, too. Up until this point Ellen Malone was merely questionable, but now she was millimeters away from being categorized as the enemy.

Then, at just the right time, she placed a temporary immunity on herself from reaching that status, but believe me she was still at the top of the watch list. "Doro, your father's discovery, the Doromium element, was the basis for the creation of the Seneca

Society. Without Doromium, *without your father*, Seneca wouldn't exist. As we began to embark upon the path of Doromium, a world of opportunity presented itself. We accepted these opportunities with the intention to create a place where great discoveries could be developed, void of political agenda, and subsequently released to the entire world."

I needed more information. I needed it fast and I needed it bad. I looked at my dad. "What does Doromium do?"

My dad pepped up. "Remember how excited I was, Doro?"

I nodded. The little girl in me remembered just how joyous my dad was when he had made the discovery after years of dedicated work. It's as happy as I ever remember him being before *POOF!* He was gone.

"It's because I found something that would change everything. The element Doromium protects living organisms from Solar Ultraviolet Radiation by creating a shield of atmosphere that settles in to fill gaps in the ozone layer, once believed to be irreparable."

I let that settle in. The implications began to race through my mind. In the Aboves people could only go outside at certain times because of the damage to the ozone layer. Farm life, marine life, the entire eco-system on the face of the planet was nose diving to its demise, and I imagined how this could change that. My dad, Ellen and Jadel all watched me coming to these realizations.

My dad went on bursting with enthusiasm, jutting his head forward and talking with his hands, "Here we are refining Doromium under pressures *hundreds of thousands* times the regular pressure of sea level. Mining, capturing, condensing, then releasing it into the atmosphere in a vapor, through Lake Titicaca."

This was the guy I knew and loved and missed more than my tiny heart could ever cope with. I wasn't surprised but I was indeed blown away.

Ellen told me, "Doro, your dad is the mastermind of Doromium."

I looked at him. His smile was tainted by knowing he had broken my heart. I had to understand though so I asked, "Why here, so hidden from everyone? Hidden from your family?"

My dad didn't take his eyes off of mine as he explained, "Doromium can only be produced on a large scale deep inside the earth under extreme pressures. I had to come here, and unfortunately, because of the secrecy of the discovery and struggle that has ensued to take control of it, you and your mom couldn't know about it."

I looked to each one of them, imagining the various pieces of information each one of them possessed, and they, in turn, looked at me as if they were waiting to see a light bulb go off. But I was still processing fresh data. If what they were saying was true, it would have been simple-minded for me to continue thinking they had taken my dad from me and that was that.

"So it is true, then. You chose chasing science over staying with mom and me."

"I chose science *for* mom and you, Doro. Every choice I've made has been based on what I believed would be best for you."

I nodded. I got it. I had made the choice, too, to leave my mom and come here because I thought it would be best for her, not because I was choosing this world over my life with her. "Kind of ironic that I lost my father to *Doro*mium, isn't it?"

Ellen softened. "You never lost your dad, Doro. He just had a job to do in order to become your hero."

"I don't need a hero. I just need my family back."

"Believe me, I want that too— so badly! I always planned on bringing you and your mother here. But the months started adding up, and then they became years."

"You could have come back for us."

"I couldn't, Doro, I would have risked all of this. I would have risked your future. That's something I could never allow to happen."

Ellen added, "Doro, the political landscape in the Aboves is so out of control right now and the struggle for power is so ruthless that we had to keep your father protected here, in Seneca."

My dad went on, "At the same time we had to keep you and mom far away from me, and the knowledge of what I was doing. Believe it or not, there was a detail assigned to you two from the day I left, and I had constant updates."

I didn't want to accept it, but I got it. On top of coming to this place of understanding my dad, so many things Ellen said and did finally clicked. She had to safeguard information while exerting integrity and levelheadedness.

My dad held my hand. "I am so proud of the person standing right here in front of me." I closed my eyes for a beat and let his praise permeate my whole being. He continued, "These times have been trying, but I promise if we stick to our guns, we will see the light at the end of this tunnel."

27

IT WAS WITH complete unease that I left my dad and headed back to where it had all begun— Hub 144, but I had to do what I had to do. My dad had asked me to go with Ellen, Senator Gilroy and Jadel. He assured me that they were on our side, dedicated to protecting us as well as Doromium, and that they'd explain more as we were on the move. I didn't know if this was the right choice or if I would ever see him again. I had to choose between answering to my wary protective mechanisms and refusing to go, or trusting my dad and this whole squad.

This trust thing seemed like it would haunt me until the end of time. Why couldn't it just be clear who I could trust? I had complete faith in my dad before he was gone, but then everything changed. Even though he had explained why he'd left my mom and me for Seneca, I didn't have certainty that what he said was true. Believe or not believe— I just wasn't ready to rest one way or the other. Nothing could change the heartbreak I went through when he disappeared, but I was relieved we were united and I wanted to keep that momentum on the up and up. I decided to comply with the urgency expressed by the group and go with the people with whom my dad had entrusted me.

I had come to know a thing or two about how valuable time was. Every second counted. Every single breath was numbered. I didn't want to overthink and play out the debate to every end because I knew it would make me crazy and I wouldn't find a definitive answer. It was as simple as this: Had I stayed, I might have gained my dad, but in turn, been far away from my Mom and Dom.

Just like the nanobots that once quantum entangled brains with a mainframe in Claytor Lake, Dom and I were two entangled souls now. No matter where each one of us was on the planet, no matter how much space and time stood between us, each of our hearts held a piece of the other. It was quite something how the thought of this made me warm and fuzzy yet empty at the same time. I missed him like crazy. I wanted him back. I resisted the urge to communicate with him via flex because I didn't want to implicate him in anything I was doing, and I definitely didn't want to call attention to the fact that he had a flex implant that could be hacked like mine was. I had asked Ellen if he and Reba were okay and back in Hub 144, and she assured me they were. At least I could have some peace in knowing that.

As I left my dad, I tried to breathe out my worries and breathe in the propensity for faith because I was not moving forward on pure facts alone. I took deep, concentrated breaths in and out as Senator Gilroy, Ellen, and Jadel accompanied me to the flighter.

We took an underground acoustic carrier inside Hub 48 to an ascension dome that, after a long ride up, deposited us in the Aboves. As per usual, it was in a heavily treed area. It was the middle of the night but still hot outside, and damp. There was an awaiting flighter with one mute driver in black.

We got in. I sat in the third of three rows and looked out. Ellen sat next to me. Senator Gilroy and Jadel got in last and sat in the middle row.

It had been quiet up until that point for everyone knew that inside a Senecan common area such as an acoustic carrier or ascension dome, anyone could be listening.

Senator Gilroy kicked off the conversation as the flighter took off. "As history has taught us," he asserted, "war will rage on endlessly for power over land. That has been the model of societal hierarchies here on earth for millennia upon millennia. What is happening now is that the old kings and queens have shifted their focus away from engaging in these petty wars of man. They have concluded that the only way you can potentially claim a new society and keep it is by settling it and creating it. Not by pitching a flag. Not by building bigger armies. No, *strength*, they have come to realize, lies in usurping knowledge. They have tackled and claimed elements, commodities, technology, and as you saw in Hub 48, a dynamic power source from deep within the earth— geodynamic power, is now on the table."

I nodded as I wondered just how much of the information coming at me Brittany already knew. Every word that came out of Senator Gilroy's mouth made complete sense. I mean, what would be the point of making up such an extravagant story? This wasn't Broadway. I had a better understanding of what my dad's life work was all about. "I don't understand the problem though." I asked, "Why would they keep Doromium from fixing the damage done to the earth if it can actually do that? Instead of just letting the earth continue to… go to hell? Who would make such a stupid decision?"

Gilroy replied, "The decision isn't actually all that 'stupid.' In fact, it was calculated in a way we want you to understand, but this understanding is a process. There are so many pieces for you to absorb that make up the whole picture—"

Ellen cut in, "And you *have* been doing that, Doro, faster than I imagine anyone ever could, let alone someone your age. I knew you'd be able to. Do you remember when I first met you and I told you I knew your potential?"

"I remember every detail of that day."

"Me, too. I didn't know exactly how, but I knew we would end up here."

Ellen was good.

Jadel was dead silent the whole time, but he was good, and so was Gilroy. They were all so darn on point I suddenly felt that in order to be a solid team, I wanted to bring what I could to the table. If you are only as good as your weakest link, there is no way I was going to be that.

Senator Gilroy continued, "Doro, I want you to think about this. If we can harvest geodynamic power, then hell, everyone should have free power, right? But the kings and queens want to monopolize and charge for it. They want to control these free elements and global resources, and the patents, and then re-sell it all to the people. Because if they control Doromium, the one hope for this world to exist, they also control everything that can destroy our world, and that secures their grasp on complete power. In conjunction with this, all of the technology in the world has been absorbed into Seneca. We've got this puppet government that believes we are operating a model for an ideal society, and granted, we are doing a pretty great job considering, but really the very few families that control Seneca will have all the patents under their umbrella. These families are very secretive— and the Wallingsfords are in this inner-circle."

"But," I said, "you said it before, and it is true: as long as there is man, there will be a struggle for power, so what can we do really?"

"You're right. But power has never been absolute. This faction inside Seneca has one agenda only and that is to realize that level of power. In order to attain it, they will ravage our Earth, deplete us of everything and leave us behind with nothing."

"But where will they go?"

"Their ultimate goal is to leave the planet and colonize Mars with all of humanity under their rule."

"No way."

Gilroy nodded as he clamped down on his lips.

As we were quiet for a beat, the notion of a great exodus to Mars filled my ether.

"Many intellectual leaders of the twenty-first century have been suggesting that going to Mars is what we need to do to survive, and, well, this is no longer just a theory. As a matter of fact, they are very close to it. But we— *Ellen, myself, your dad*, and many others, don't want to abandon the earth and fellow brothers and sisters that don't make the choice to follow. We want to take care of our planet. We want to repair and build a better, more harmonious life for everyone here," he said. "We believe in championing diversity of thought, whereas they believe in: *think like us, join the Departers and follow us to the promised land... or stay behind and see the end.* To us *this* is the land of promise."

"There's no way they can get away with that."

Ellen was quick to respond, "I used to say things like that too, Doro. But one thing I know for sure. In Seneca, if something is even remotely possible, don't disregard it."

Gilroy painted the big picture. "The goal of the Repairers is to use the Earth's resources to repair the earth. We want to keep digging deeper and deeper to access more resources and to stop using fossil fuels which are destroying our atmosphere. The Earth's electromagnetic energy needs to be affordable to the people, and Doromium should be released to repair what has been destroyed. Right now, Doro, your dad's discovery is being weaponized, and *you* are being weaponized." Gilroy was the first person I'd met in Seneca that wasn't giving me bits and pieces of information through ambiguous comments. He was an information man, and I was a data girl. The Gilroys were my kind of people.

Ellen added, "The game has changed, Doro. You changed the game by challenging the deceit."

Ellen wasn't against me— she wasn't against me at all. All along I'd been unsure. She hadn't been simply playing both sides of the fence as I'd assumed. She was doing what she had to do, making political moves with a solid head on her shoulders, and I just didn't have the information to comprehend that before today. Knowing what I knew now, I realized yet again how much more there was to know and that I needed to keep not only my eyes and ears open, but my mind as well.

"So, then, it's settled," I said with conviction.

Gilroy's eyebrows lifted, eager for further explanation, but the look on Ellen's face said it all. She knew I was familiar with addition, and this was all adding up. It was about to go down.

"We have to stop them!" I exclaimed and then inquired, "I assume you have a plan?"

Ellen replied very bluntly. I'd heard this strong tone from her several times before, one being the first time we met. It's what earned her my respect to begin with. "You have an illegal implant and it's been hacked once before. You might have solved that problem for the time being, Doro, but now that you've got the implant inside your brain, you are always going to be susceptible to attacks. I warned you of this in the debate."

"I like to learn the hard way."

"Yes, well, that's also how you've compromised the big picture."

I knew what she was getting at, and I was prepared to assume responsibility. "I am sorry if you think my choice to get the implant was irresponsible. But you made it, too, once."

"I had a much different set of parameters guiding my decision, and I clearly don't mean as much to the other side as you do. They know what you mean to your dad. They know that he's given up everything for you and your future. They know your mind is equally as brilliant as his."

"Fair enough," I said. "I don't quite believe I am as smart as my dad, but it is becoming more clear to me, the part that I play in all of this. So what matters now is that we get to the bottom of who did it, we expose them to everyone and I reclaim jurisdiction over my own mind."

Senator Gilroy nodded. "That's the right idea, Doro."

Ellen added, "But we can't get ahead of ourselves. This isn't about exposing. This about counterintelligence and understanding. Step one is that we find out the workings of the enemy. That means, identify exactly who placed this virus on you, exactly how, and exactly why. We need to get to the bottom of who planted it and identify their goals."

Senator Gilroy agreed. "Ellen is right. This is a matter of knowing thy enemy."

I agreed, too. "There is only one way I know how to make that happen. I do know a thing or two about working backwards with coding inside a hack to identify a source. But the problem is, I don't have the tools I need."

"Which are?" Gilroy asked.

"Computing systems advanced enough for me to reinstate the bug that was wiped from my implant."

"We can make that happen," Ellen assured me.

Gilroy wasn't sold on me handling this alone. "We can assign you a team—"

"No team," I replied. "I need solitude and focus."

Gilroy looked to Ellen. "She's got this," Ellen assured Gilroy. "Any outsiders would only meddle in her process."

I asserted, "I've made it inside all of the most secure gambling sites across the world, I've cracked the Iranian Ministry of Defense Systems, and I uncovered the Necrolla

Carne conspiracy inside Seneca. I can do this."

"Alright then," Gilroy said, and I sensed relief by the sigh in his voice. He didn't know me well enough to know I didn't need much convincing for techie games of cat and mouse.

"I will find these suckers." I was certain.

Ellen smiled. "I love your enthusiasm, Doro. I know your father explained to you the importance of fragmented information and never, ever telling another soul what is going on."

"Of course."

"In a way, you are untouchable, but that level of untouchability doesn't extend to your friends or even your mom. There is just too much at stake, and the reality is if they know too much, they'll be taken out without impunity. Your boyfriend, Dom, and your friend, Reba. There will be no hesitation."

I knew it was true. "I get it. They know my relationships, they know all of our relationships, don't they?"

Senator Gilroy and Ellen both nodded, and she said, "We know there is an enemy, but we don't know the scope and reaches of that enemy."

Not if I could help it. "It's time to find out."

Ellen nodded. "Yes it is. Keep your friends close," and I finished her thought, "but your enemies closer. The only way to do that is to go into the eye of the storm."

My mind churned at full speed. This suddenly felt exhilarating in a way I'd been missing. It was as if 'old me' was here with 'new me' brewing the perfect combination of fire and confidence for 'future me.' "I will lure them in and we will see their cards."

The flighter made a smooth landing on a simple runway in a remote part of the Peruvian jungle.

Unlike LAX or Dulles, the two airports I had taken off from and landed at the last time around, this runway had no physical building on it. It was a pop-up runway of sorts lined with lavender lights and there was only this one BoomJet on the runaway when we showed up. Senator Gilroy, Ellen, Jadel and I boarded the BoomJet.

I braced myself in the black rubber seat as the engine powered up with that breathtaking deep whir that massaged my bones. My second-ever BoomJet flight was about to take off and it borderline excited me as much as the first, only this time I knew where I was going and what I had to do.

28

THIS TIME THE BoomJet landed not at Dulles Airport, but on a hidden runway edging up to the heavily populated domain of Northern Virginia. Night had pushed us into the wee hours of day— a time I had fallen in love with without realizing it when it happened. These early mornings blew a peace into me that nights too often stole. I associated dark hours with battles for sleep, whereas sunrise was synonymous with fresh starts. I could take on the world the way I wanted to instead of the world taking me on. Don't get me wrong. I was a Cali girl for life, but this morning, moody, blue-gray-skied Virginia took me by the hand and the heart and welcomed me back.

It was cool and quiet as I stepped off the BoomJet into the lush green landscape that instantaneously engulfed my whole being. I held on tight to the moments between each step down to the tarmac, finding inside each breath an infinite space to do cartwheels. If only I had known how to do cartwheels. A girl can dream. I was ready to rock Seneca and find justice for my father's dream, and life on our beautiful, broken, betrayed planet.

We took a flighter from the BoomJet into the golden ring location in Great Falls where I had come for my very first journey into the glorious Seneca City.

When we were parked, Senator Gilroy, Ellen and I stepped out of the flighter, but Jadel did not. Ellen and Gilroy both said their piece to Jadel, and Jadel said his to them, then Ellen and Gilroy moved on like it was the obvious time to part with him. But for some reason I hesitated. It was as if my heart told me Jadel was supposed to stay with us. I looked back through the door at him, confounded. We spoke only through our energy.

He nodded and smiled at me.

I nodded and smiled back. Never did I imagine I could feel a real connection with someone in S.O.I.L. There was still so much mystery, so much left unsaid, yet we understood something deep about each other. It didn't make sense on paper. I still had so much to learn about this guy, but my heart fed me the words to say nonetheless, "Thank you."

I leaned into the flighter and hugged him, then backed away looking at him. He gave me a nod as he squinted his eyes and quietly said, "The gratitude is mine."

I'd never forget that emerald sparkle. I turned and followed Ellen and Gilroy to the golden ring. When I looked back over my shoulder, the flighter was gone. My stomach sank because I didn't know if Jadel and I were just two passing ships and that was that, or if we'd meet again one day.

There was a man in black waiting for us at the golden ring. We went through the motions of entering the ring, being encased in the glowing iridescent dome, and descended into the earth.

By the time I was back in the heart of Seneca City the morning bustle was alive and kicking. The ghost sensation of Reba greeting me for the first time darted through me and it brought joy to my soul. I loved it here. I loved the people, I loved the place, I loved the possibility. I couldn't go on living knowing I didn't do everything in my power to protect that.

"Welcome home," Ellen said.

I was about to lose my mind again, but by choice this time. I wanted to see my mom before that, knowing it could very well be the last time, but believing in myself that I would do everything in my power to make sure it wasn't.

"It's good to be back."

"I bet it is."

Senator Gilroy put his hands on each of our shoulders. "If you two will excuse me, I want to get a chance to give my daughter a hug before her day of sessions begins."

"Of course. And please give her one for me as well," Ellen replied.

"And me," I added.

"Will do." He turned to me. "Ellen knows how to be in touch with me if you need anything."

"Thank you," I said.

"Get some sleep and Godspeed to you both." With that, off he went.

Ellen looked to me. "I'm sure there are a few people you want to see as well."

"It's crazy. I haven't had a moment to actually enjoy the fact that I have my mom here. I want to do that this morning."

"You do that. We have a long road ahead, starting bright and early tomorrow morning."

"Okay."

I suddenly felt sorry for Ellen, wondering whom she would go see. I knew she didn't have any loved ones here. Ellen had to leave people behind in the Aboves, too, including her son, Connor. I knew how hard that was for her and I hoped one day soon she would be reunited with him. She had buried herself in her work, but I pondered if that ever got to her. I couldn't imagine that those feelings could just be squashed. With no family in Seneca, with whom did she connect, whom did she love? "Who will you go see today?" I asked.

A hint of sadness washed across her face, but it was gone in a flash. "Too much to get done, there's no time to socialize today. I'll pick you up in the morning."

Ellen forced a smile, then turned and went.

I watched her go for a moment before I headed to the main citizen residences where my mom had her place. I was so excited to see her and hug her and hear about her first month in Seneca City. I wished I had been there for all of her firsts— especially her first Ty's Sushi experience!

I got to her door, knocked, and waited.

After a few moments the door opened.

"Hi, Mom."

"Doro!" She threw her arms around me. "Oh my god. Doro."

"Campbell." A man's voice said with way too much pep.

I looked behind my mom.

Gregory Zaffron!? "What are you doing here?" I snapped.

My mom was confused by my reaction. "Whoa, honey, it's okay. This is Gregory."

"I know. Wait." I shook my head in disbelief, trying to shake off the shock. "How is this happening, how do you two even know each other?"

This wasn't how this moment was supposed to go. This couldn't be. Not now when we were so close to being back together as a family.

"Great to see you, too," Gregory smirked.

"They sent Gregory to notify me after you disappeared, and he has been nice enough to stop by to check on me ever since," my mom said, smiling back at Gregory. Totally clueless.

No.

No!

No!!!

I wasn't seeing this. Oh god, please tell me my flex implant had already slipped back into the hack and I was hallucinating and this couldn't be! It was. It *was* happening! Gregory Zaffron befriending my mom! My entire world was suddenly crushed by a boulder. But I held back every bit of emotion I could, keeping it all held tightly inside in a little box so Gregory couldn't see that he affected me.

My mom didn't take her eyes off of me. "I don't understand," she said, and looked to Gregory. "If it wasn't for his concern, I would have been all alone here, Doro."

"She's right, kiddo,"

"Don't call me kiddo!"

"Whoa, relax tiger." Gregory reached for my elbow, and I yanked away. "I just want to make sure your mom is okay. You've had us worried sick," he said, all fake nice.

Us?! I couldn't stand another second. All I could do was turn away and take a huge breath as I felt all the oxygen inside of me had been sucked out.

I couldn't tell my mom that my dad was alive. I wanted to turn around and scream it so bad. So, so bad. To announce at the top of my lungs that my dad would be back for us after he had saved the world. But in the moments just before I walked away from my dad, he had said, "The only way to keep your mother safe is to keep her out of it." I heard his words echo in my head. He wanted to protect her, and here she was being duped by this scumbag, Gregory. The exact opposite of what my dad wanted.

"Excuse us for a moment, Gregory," my mom said and she stepped outside the door with me. She commanded it to close. I kept my back to her. I couldn't bear to look at her. She stood behind me and took my hand. My impulse was to pull away.

We were alone in the big empty hallway. The doors to the residences were flush with the walls, which were all stark gray and that suddenly felt ironic because we were in some crazy gray area. It hit me that my mom and I were perpetually stuck in an undefinable hallway to somewhere else. It hurt so bad that our liberation was within reach, but then, in the blink of an eye, it slipped further away than it was before. There was nothing I could do to bring us closer, even though I was standing there with her.

"Doro. He's just been a friend. Nothing to freak out about."

I shook my head. I didn't want to hear any more about this. I just wanted it to stop. I turned around to face her. "He's no friend of ours, Mom. Don't be fooled."

"Okay, you know what? Who cares about *him?* Where have you been?! Where?! I came here to be with you and then you were gone."

I couldn't shake this image of Gregory acting buddy-buddy with my mom. There were such sickening ulterior motives going on that I couldn't explain to her and I wanted to puke. Instead, I stood up straight and took a stance. "I've been on my own now for a while in Seneca and I'm going to be making major choices as an adult now, too."

I could see this stung my mom. I was her only child, telling her I was a child no longer. This wasn't tit for tat, though it might have appeared that way. She looked intently at me as I continued, "There are some things going on here that you can't know about, that you won't understand, and I am committing my life from this point forward to fighting for what is right."

All I really wanted to say was that Dad was alive and that he and I were going to fix everything and all be back together, but I couldn't and it killed me. Dad was alive and she could have him back soon but she was closing that door. This was horrendous and could be an absolute disaster.

"I wish you wouldn't do this."

"And I wish you wouldn't do *that*," I motioned towards Gregory.

My mom clamped her lips and shook her head.

"Well… I guess at this point we each do what is right for ourselves. So good for you, you're not lonely anymore," I said before turning and walking away.

"I love you, Doro," she said quietly. I didn't stop and say it back and I think that actually hurt me more than it hurt her.

29

BECAUSE IT WASN'T safe to flex, I went straight to the youth residences to look for Dom, but he wasn't there. Of course he wasn't. Session had just started. I knew I would find no such desired results by going to Reba's either, because he was most certainly in session, too. To make matters worse, he was probably in the Aboves for the rest of the morning, on some on-location Intuerian assignment, so I wouldn't get to see him before I set out to Claytor Lake with Ellen.

My breath was short, my heart raced, and my hands were jittery. This was awful. I couldn't get the image of my mom and her 'buddy' Gregory out of my head. The skin around my eyes was raw from crying after I left my mom's place and I just couldn't undo this terrible clenching in my gut. I wiped my sweaty palms across my pants. This was not the mood I needed to be in before entering a serious neurological undertaking. All I had wanted to do was see my mom and spend some real moments with her, reconnecting and hearing about how much she loved exploring Seneca. But now I didn't want to hear anything about that. Not at all! I knew enough to know it was freaking gross.

I leaned back against the wall next to Dom's door and just sank to the floor. My stomach had dropped there before the rest of my body. My forehead rested on my knees and a toxic moan bubbled up from within the depths of me. My chest was filled with the sack of filth I'd just witnessed, but I wasn't going to let myself cry any longer. Gregory Zaffron could not have that control over me. I had already beat him fair and square, but he was coming back for more. Bringing my mom into this was just plain fighting dirty.

I was going to wait here until Dom got back.

After quite some time, a body plunked down next to me.

I didn't want to look.

My breath stopped at the top of an inhale.

"Campbella," rolled off his tongue.

I released my breath and on my next inhale, as I lifted my head, a spark of joy dropped in my lap. I threw my arms around Reba and practically knocked him over.

"Hey, chica! Happy to see you, too!"

I didn't want to let go. It felt so darn good to have him with me. My mind, body and soul full-on grabbed this guy and sucked up the cup of positivity inside of me that had been dumped out at my mom's door moments ago. I squeezed him so hard. "Thank god you're here. I thought you'd be in session."

"Yeah, well, according to my schedule I should be there but I had something else in mind."

"You knew. Of course you knew."

"And you know I'm always here for you."

"I do," I said, still squeezing him. "What happened to you guys after we split up? Is Dom okay? And Anika?"

"We parted ways with Anika in Lima, and don't know what happened to her because we flew old school jet back to Dulles, and she stayed to catch another flight. But I think she is okay."

"I hope so." That stressed me out, not knowing.

"Don't worry," Reba said, and he was right. Anika was tough and smart and would want me to stay positive. "And Dom is putting on a face like he's fine, but he's freaking out until he knows you're back."

"I wonder where he is. He should be home by now; sessions are out."

"I am actually not sure." Reba was surprised with himself. "But I do know what we should do in the meantime," he said with delight in his voice.

We gave each other knowing grins.

Half an hour later Reba and I were sitting across from each other over two steaming hot plates of chilaquiles.

"I knew we were going to be friends from the moment we met," I said to him and took my first bite. My eyes closed and my soul instantly warmed up. The lime. The cilantro. The green chile sauce. Heaven!

"And I knew even before that," he replied with a whole body kind of smile.

"Thank you, Reba... for everything."

"You don't need to thank me. Isn't this just what friends do?"

I nodded and looked at him as I chewed. This guy was so genuine, it killed me. I mean, how incredible would the world be if there were more people like Reba in it? Innocent, yet full of wisdom, love, loyalty and so dang cute, too.

I swallowed my bite and all I could think to say to him was, "I love you."

Reba blushed. He wasn't shocked to hear it from my mouth because I was sure he already knew I loved him, and I knew that he loved me, too. I guess you could say I was part Intuerian when I was around Reba.

"I love you, too, Campbella."

He hadn't touched his food yet and half of mine was already halfway digested and on its way to the poo-renew system to make more energy for this advanced society. "Watch out, Reebs. If you don't eat that, I will."

He pushed his fork around his plate, but clearly didn't have an appetite and couldn't hide his state of unease.

"Maybe we need to go get you a tuna sandwich and a cookie?"

That got a smile out of him, but he kept his eyes on the plate of food.

"What's up?" I asked.

"I just feel... worried about you."

"I can tell, and I realize we're going to have to talk about this."

He looked up at me with those puppy dog eyes. "Don't do it, Doro."

I put my fork down, and with the softest tone I could find in me, I tried to let him down easy. "I don't have a choice."

"You always have a choice."

"Well, then, this has to be it."

"But you're making a choice without knowing all the facts."

"I thought facts weren't what you dabbled in."

"Here's the thing—"

"You think I haven't thought long and hard about this?"

"I know you have."

"I could just stay as is and do nothing about what I now know. Yeah, sure, I'll remember meeting my dad but what good does that do me in this world? We still won't all get to be together. Beyond that, there is too much riding on this... I can't get into the details, Reebs, I think you know that."

Reba nodded his head with an annoyed little scrunch in his lips. So I added, "You know what you know, I know what I know, and that's just the nature of the beast."

"I understand."

"Do you also understand that my inaction would be a detriment to the whole society?"

I could tell that he got that. But something else was playing into his visible emotions. Doubt filled his drooping eyes.

I continued, "When I go through with this I will forget meeting my dad and all that transpired down there in Hub 48, but we *will* meet again— as long as I stay on this path."

"There are many paths. You have to be careful which one you choose to go down."

I sat forward. "Reba, I am sorry this feels unsettling to you, but to me it is exactly what I need to do."

"I understand your motivation, Campbella, I really do. But I just want you to consider this. Your soul will always be, but *where* it goes could be in jeopardy with the decisions you make right now."

I had made my mind up, but he was really insistent in his opinion and I wanted to understand why. "Okay. Please explain."

"So, your soul exists inside you and outside of you at the same time, right?"

He was speaking a foreign language to me, but I had to listen to my friend, because if anyone was fluent in this language, I knew it would be Reba. I sat back, placed my hands in my lap and peeled open the door to my mind.

"You are right here with me. We are both experiencing this living, breathing consciousness together, largely in part because of the quantum mechanics inside our brains that serve as a vehicle for our consciousness here on earth. Right?"

"I'm with you. I'm going to finish my plate while you continue to explain. And, if *you're* not careful, I will finish yours next."

He pushed his plate in my direction. "You mess with the inner-workings of your brain, you could also mess with your consciousness— and without consciousness, this experience here, as you know it, will cease to exist. Your soul will find its way out into the great wide open, and your human body will become nothing more than a robot... or dust in the wind."

The gravity of Reba's wisdom tugged at my certainty. He didn't want to lose what we had here— an organically grown fondness for one another's beating heart. While I got it, I believed that potentially losing our connection, along with all the other great relationships I had built, was the gamble I had to take.

30

"Good morning, Doro. You ready to go?"

It was par for the course that Ellen arrived spot-on-time at seven in the morning. I lugged myself through the door, hadn't even brushed my hair. "This is where I say *I was born ready*, right?" I pushed a smile through, wishing I could pretend I was bright-eyed and bushy-tailed, but the truth emanated from my heavy eyelids like a dense fog.

"Too bad you weren't able to get a good night's rest before your big day," Ellen said.

"This is where I wish I could say *sleep is overrated*. But it's not. I would kill for some sleep right now." I couldn't sleep because after my meal with Reba, I went back to wait for Dom outside his residence. I wasn't going to flex him and have anyone monitoring us, so I just waited and waited. Dom didn't return to his room by the time the acoustic carriers stopped running to my residence hall, so I had to take the last ride home without seeing him.

"You just have a lot on your mind," Ellen said. "A little more than the average teenager, I'd say."

"Yeah. Totally the opposite of my childhood when I didn't have a care in the world. That just feels like a distant memory now."

We were both quiet for a moment as we walked to the acoustic carrier. I kept thinking about it, though— how life was astronomically harder now. "Jeez, those were easier times. How is it that we all thought it was so tough? We had it good."

Ellen smiled. "You wouldn't be the first to wish for going back to when times were easier. Life is hard for a lot of people right now. Humanity is suffering deeply on so many levels, and it will take a tremendous force to heal us."

"It's just so sad."

"Indeed it is, but, Doro, you just remember our goal is to bring everyone with us into better times and I think you'll muster up all the energy you need to carry through and be instrumental in seeing to it that that happens."

I tried to be mindful of that. All too often I was wrapped up in *me* like a little cocoon. What was happening to *me*, what had happened to *me*, and what was going to happen to *me*? I had to find a balance between doing this for me *and* the collective good, not just one or the other. Truth is, although I wanted peace and love to prevail on earth, I wasn't a pawn in anyone's game. I was human and I wanted my family back, too.

Ellen and I were en route to The Center for Quantum Neurology and Consciousness Experimentations at Claytor Lake, otherwise referred to as C-QNCE. It was a part of that secretive hub I had yet to see and I was excited, to say the least, but I also knew I needed to stay vigilant. I sat back in my seat in the flighter and got strapped in. As we flighted along, I thought about everything that was going on. Ellen quietly jotted notes on her FlexBoard.

My challenge had grown in the past twenty-four hours. Not only did I have the whole enemy-of-the-Repairers I was preparing to take down, but now I also had this issue with my mom. She was moving on right before my eyes. Now that I was away from Seneca City and my mom, it left more space for her relationship with Gregory to progress and that horrified me to no end. I swallowed and a lump formed in my throat. I was the only one who could stop their connection from fully blossoming before it was too late. I didn't want to even imagine what "too late" looked like. Chills shot up my spine and I literally shivered. Would I feel different when I forget my dad is alive?

Rather than dwelling in the dismal abyss of my thoughts, I shifted to soak up the world outside of my head. The plump spinachy land that Ellen and I traveled through wasn't just a backdrop painted by Mother Nature. It was a bathtub for the soul and I needed a soak.

Spring was alive and kicking on the east coast and, coming

from a lifetime in the desert, the musky, thick air was still a novelty to me. I ran my fingers up my arm to feel how moisturized my skin felt. It was like silk. My racing mind slowed. I remembered to be aware of my breaths, a practice my mom taught me.

"We're going to see a Quantum Neurologist under the premise of a follow-up on your *brain aneurysm*," Ellen said. "Short of political details, she has top secret clearance enough to know the bio-tech reality behind the cover, and why we must do this procedure, but her crew does not know any details, or who you are. They will be following her instructions. So just keep that in mind and answer all questions accordingly. I'll do the majority of the talking."

"Got it."

Ellen Malone always knew what she wanted and where she was going. I had to give her that. She never gave the impression that she was confused or even trying to figure things out, while she kept information close to the vest like a champion. She was a real mentor in this sense. But I was confused as to how it was even possible for this to be allowed, considering I was still a minor. "Ellen, how is it that they are even allowed to operate on me like this, without my mom's consent?"

"In order for you to become a Senecan as a minor without a parent also joining, your mother had to sign a lot of legal documentations. One of the releases was an 'in loco parentis' for me, so that in the event I couldn't contact her and you were under emergency medical care, I would be the one to make decisions."

"Hmm." I pondered that. Of course my mom made sure I would get the medical attention I needed. She had told me Ellen would act as my guardian when it came to certain things, but this just seemed too major to be allowed.

"But does the 'in loco parentis' really still apply considering my mom is in Seneca now?"

"Because it is tied to something top secret in nature, yes."

It wasn't exactly comforting to know that someone other than my parents could make these sorts of decisions regarding my mental and physical states, but if it was going to be anyone, I could accept that it was Ellen. She and my dad were on the same page.

As we descended inside the dome to the fantastic Claytor Lake hub, I felt exhilaration seep into my bloodstream. It was about to go down, and down we went. How ironic.

Yesterday's chat with Reba resurfaced in my mind. Yeah, I had confidence in my capabilities to reverse engineer quantum computing formulas, but it wasn't as clean as me hacking gambling websites. This was my brain we were talking about. What if he was right about this whole soul thing? What if I was handing my brain over to be a guinea pig for Seneca and that had ramifications beyond my skill jurisdiction? The reality was that I was the golden girl here, the one player currently up to bat. "The plan" to defeat "the Departers mission" took precedence above all else.

A gray-haired woman in her sixties greeted us the moment our ascension dome opened to the Claytor Lake hub. This woman looked like a boss. She wore a fitted, powder blue lab coat, gray pants and a FlexScope around her neck. She had a team behind her— four young men and a woman in white coats.

"Ellen Malone and Dorothy Campbell, I presume?"

Ellen extended her hand. "It is such a pleasure."

"Dr. Renee Cairncross. The pleasure is mine."

I loved that worldly British accent and her husky voice. But I recalled Dr. Kulkarni had pulled one over on me at first sight with his doctor's coat, worldly accent, and kind old eyes, and he turned out to be Gregory Zaffron's go-to doctor for erasing people's memories inside Seneca before they were banished to the Aboves.

Ellen turned to me. "We are in good hands here, Doro. Dr. Cairncross is a phenomenal doctor. She went to one of the best schools in the world— Oxford."

Dr. Cairncross was quick to add, "American-educated as well, my dear. I went for my PhD at The University of Maryland."

"Nice," I said. I could play the flattery game, for now, but what school she went to didn't mean squat to me. "I should be applying to college right about now, but, well—"

Ellen gave me a look and continued, "Dr. Cairncross started out in anesthesiology before moving deeper into applied consciousness studies when she came to the United States."

One of her team members, a slender young man, maybe twenty-five years old, stepped forward, right next to Dr. Cairncross and added, "Only to become the world's leading expert on quantum neurology and consciousness."

Her accolades were impressive, but let's be real. They didn't give me the certainty I needed to hand my brain over to an experiment. This wasn't biology. I wasn't a frog.

"Shall we?" Dr. Cairncross asked.

Reba's warnings resounded in my head. I wasn't moving forward with a sense that this was all safe and sound, but I trepidatiously nodded and would continue in this direction while looking out for red flags every single step of the way. Ellen put her hand up as if to say, "Let's go."

With Ellen on one side and me on the other, Dr. Cairncross escorted us through the colossal complex of doctors, scientists, technologists and scholars collaborating in the symphony of genius that I admired. The doctor's team trailed behind us, all typing notes on their pads and scurrying along to keep a tight follow on their leader. Truth be told, I was terrified, but this sort of erudite arrangement mitigated my anxieties to a degree.

I kept my mouth shut out of respect for what I was witnessing, and also in order to keep my eyes and ears wide open to recieve information. We happened to retrace the steps I had taken when I came here for the Necrolla Carne vaccine upon my induction into Seneca. I realized this was about the same time in the morning that I had come back when I had seen Dom helping the man in his regenerative medicine session. As we came upon that very location, I noticed a group of scholars working on the other side of the glass wall and there was Dom!

My heartbeat jumped and I stopped in my tracks. One of Dr. Cairncross's assistants bumped into me and dropped his pad. Everyone stopped.

"Sorry." I picked the pad back up for him. He swiped it from my hand, annoyed, and resumed what he was doing. I looked back up at Dom, but it wasn't Dom at all. For milliseconds my mind had played a trick on me, where I felt like I was a stone's throw away from him but, in reality, we were countless miles apart.

My body snapped to and continued to follow the group while my heart melted into a puddle on the floor right then and there. I blinked and I was under the ice cold rapids at Difficult Run with Dom, but the muffled sounds of Dr. Cairncross talking and feet walking wouldn't let me stay there. As we rounded a corner, my attention snapped back to the present. My hand was on the necklace Dom had given me, rubbing the moonstone to soothe my aching heart and worried mind.

A shiny white wall opened at the end of the hall and we

entered what seemed like a transitional area. The wall closed back up and the eight of us stood inside a small cube-shaped room, shiny white on all sides including the floor. It was claustrophobic but I knew this moment would quickly pass. A light beamed over us and the moment it turned off, the wall opened on the other side of the room.

31

OUR GROUP, CONSISTING of Ellen, Dr. Cairncross, her assistants and myself, walked into the center of an oval laboratory that encompassed maybe five thousand square feet. The walls that encapsulated us were constructed of big, dark gray limestone bricks that they called, "Hokie Stone." It rang modern, yet archaic, haunting in a way, and there was a chill in the air which I used to my advantage. I swallowed a shot of invigoration.

In the middle of the room there was a vessel with glowing, lightly bubbling, clear liquid inside. It was similar in size and shape to the BioNan. Maybe a bit larger, like the size of a personal flighter vehicle, upright. There was a hefty chair next to it with a screen connected to an arm— all sleek, black on black, and it sat on wheels. Instinctively, I was wary but treated this room and its contents with a calm respect, as did Ellen.

The mixture of excitement and nerves rendered me silent but I think on the outside I appeared deceivingly calm.

I was increasingly fascinated by the brain and was arriving

into a greater awareness of its unparalleled complexity set off by my experience with the flex implant. These brains of ours weren't merely some gelatinous, melon-sized gobs that made us think and instructed our bodies to move. I was on the cusp of realizing firsthand just a wild bit more of what the brain was capable of, and what we were capable of doing with it, particularly when paired with technology.

I took a moment to acknowledge that I, Doro Campbell, had been inducted into a place where the mastery of the inner-workings of the mind was underway. The notion of that grabbed me by the collar of my shirt and lifted me to my toes. I absorbed every detail in my periphery. The monitors powered up and prepped for procedure, the doctor's assistants focused on their work. In order for me to move forward, I needed to fully recognize myself as an active participant in all of this rather than letting the cynic in me think I was simply some experimental game. I looked at each individual. These people were not here to play games. Seneca was not a game. Dr. Cairncross wasn't some player here to brainwash or fool me. I mean, yeah, the thought crossed my mind more than once, but come on, who would I be fooling besides myself to believe such an elaborate set-up as this would have been created to trick me?

One of Dr. Cairncross's assistants FlexCommanded a bench to rise from the ground. "Please sit here," he said to Ellen and me, while keeping an eye on his pad and not sparing his gaze on us for even a second. So we sat. He then commanded another bench to rise diagonally next to us and the five assistants took a seat as well. I didn't know each of their respective functions, but I eyed each one and wondered.

Dr. Cairncross took a seat in the sleek black tech seat and rode it right up in front of Ellen and me. It was wild— she didn't even touch a control.

"Ms. Campbell, Ms. Malone. Welcome to the Center for Quantum Neurology and Consciousness Experimentations."

Ellen quickly replied, "It is an honor to be here with you and your team."

Something about being with an esteemed British doctor made me want to enunciate, "Thank you."

With a single hand motion, Dr. Cairncross pulled up a 3D holographic orb control from the arm of her sleek black tech seat.

"This is the NeuroQuE," Dr. Cairncross said, allowing a moment for us to absorb its unique beauty. "It is the only one of its kind in the world."

Now the BioNan was cool, but there certainly were more than one of those. Dr. Cairncross looked to me. "This machine is much more powerful than a BioNan, which I understand you are acquainted with considering you have the flex implant."

I nodded. "What does it do?"

"It has a wide scope of functions. The one which we will

utilize today is a process that, in simple terms, deletes current memories and information in the brain and restores it with a back-up from a previous date. This restoration is not a copy of brain function, it is the data contained throughout the brain."

The pit of my stomach growled. I suddenly appreciated my simple life of lame calculus tests back in my Culver City public school that I'd so desperately wanted to get away from.

"How is it even possible to safely manipulate memories like that?" I asked.

"Quadrillions of operations occur per second per neuron, and the NeuroQuE precisely retraces all of them from your visual cortex to amygdala and so on and so forth. Today we will restore your neurological data to where it was on, the 20th of May. Does that put the scope in perspective?"

I nodded with a straight face. "That's some heavy-duty processing."

Dr. Cairncross finally cracked a smile.

Still, I had to know. "So, you're saying that as long as the bug still exists in my Veil back-ups, you'll be able to just re-set me to that state and—"

"Not *if* the bug still exists. It absolutely still exists. I am looking right now, at the back-up made on 20th May," Dr. Cairncross said with certainty.

"What?" I suddenly felt naked. Nobody could access my Veil, and she just had. "How did you access my Veil?"

Dr. Cairncross looked up from her screen. "Firstly, Miss Campbell, I can commend you on your brilliance as exhibited in the Aboves, but the range of your skills thus far may only be measured by the tools you have been given. This will change. Secondly, it is crucial to understand that privacy is a commodity in this subjective experience of ours. It can be bought and sold, it is never permanent and *never* guaranteed."

I swallowed hard. Dr. Cairncross breezed right on into my Veil without blinking an eye. The bug hit me on May 20th— the day I landed in Peru and went to the outfitter in Lima. What Ellen and Senator Gilroy had said was piecing together. Someone absolutely knew I was getting close to my dad and rather than letting that happen, they distorted and manipulated my reality in an effort to deliver me into the hands of the enemy. But then Jadel showed up. It made total sense. Exactly who was responsible, though? It was clearer than ever: There was only one way to find out, and I was going to do it.

I chomped at the bit to understand the technological process before I closed my eyes and relinquished control, so I proceeded with my inquisition. "Then after we identify the culprit, you can immediately bring me back to the present version of my brain?"

"Correct," Dr. Cairncross answered in a flash. "First, we shall make a near instantaneous deletion of all memories since the 31st of May. We will transfer the most recent, non-bug-infected copy from your Veil back in. This will include everything from speech to motor skills to language."

"What about my memories?"

"Good question. You see, your memories are stored all throughout your brain. Through a complex system of EEG and multi-functional lasers that measure and decipher neuronal firing, the NeuroQuE will detect the patterns that make up your memories and make duplicate copies of them. Then, when you come back, to put it in simple terms, it will shock the brain and replant those specific patterns and clusters of neuronal data."

She looked at me as if this was a walk in the park. "Okay?" she asked.

This was crazy. Or maybe it was just the new normal that life had become some techno-neurological Wild West and we were at the forefront. But I wanted to protect my memories from the gun battles. I wanted to be the one to hold them and cherish them and replant them on my own, in private.

"Who will have access to my memories? I mean, aren't you, and this whole place, under the watch of S.O.I.L.?"

Dr. Cairncross let out a small chuckle. "Of course, we shant ever deny our interminable relationship to intelligence. But, even if anyone, myself and S.O.I.L. included, were interested in your memories, they couldn't decipher any of it. Only your brain can decipher your memories because they are made possible by working in conjunction with every other piece of data in the history of your brain, and in my opinion there is no such technology that would make it possible for someone to tell you otherwise."

We all sat in a beat of silence. This. Was. Heavy.

"Shall we proceed?" Dr. Cairncross asked as she reversed her chair next to the NeuroQuE. I could tell by her tone she was a bit irritated by the fact that I was questioning her, but she wasn't the one going under, so I didn't feel bad in the least bit.

Ellen looked to me and nodded.

I was as ready as I'd ever be, "We shall."

I stood up. I got light headed recognizing that I was on the verge of relinquishing my own mind control here, "Wait."

I closed my eyes. I played back all my doubts. The room spun. There was no right or wrong answer here. There was always the chance that these people were about to put me under and turn me into some cyborg, but the sum of all parts said the odds were that they were on my team and we had to keep playing the game. I couldn't turn back. I couldn't forfeit. I focused my eyes back on the prize— revealing the deception of the Departers, bringing the greatness of Seneca discoveries to the world, and bringing my family back together.

Everyone's attention was on me, awaiting the go ahead. I took a huge breath. "Okay. Let's do this."

One of Dr. Cairncross' assistants stood up. "I'm Doctor's NeuroQuE tech, Richard. I will be giving you the directives."

The guy was as monotonous as a loaf of white bread. He

clearly took his position very seriously, though, and for that I was grateful. I could be down with a loaf of bread if it kept me safe.

"It has been a pleasure," Dr. Cairncross said with a grin. I detected under her calm and stoic demeanor that she was excited with the undertaking at hand. Before I could reply, her chair backed away as she engaged with her screen.

Another "assistant," a thin, dirty-blond guy with a French accent stood up from the bench. "I'm Nurse Beauchemin. I'll show you to the lab where we will get you hooked up for vitals and go over risks."

"Great."

We were off, but not too far. The lab happened to be in a cubicle that opened along the brick wall. There were all sorts of systems and monitors. My nerves were popping off like Mexican jumping beans.

Nurse Beauchemin handed me a bag that contained a set of white silicone underwear, a tube of gel and a cap. "I'll give you some time to change and cover all of your skin in this gel, and then I will connect you to our system and you will return to Dr. Cairncross and Richard for the procedure."

"Okay."

"You can put all of your belongings in the bag." He didn't leave the room; he just turned around.

I had to spontaneously come to terms with losing not only my mental privacy here but my physical privacy, too, because in order to enter the NeuroQuE machine I had to remove all of my clothing and lather my entire body in a freezing cold gel. *And* I basically had to be in front of everyone half-naked. I took off the necklace that Dom had given me, knowing that I would forget that beautiful moment we'd shared when he gave it to me.

I pulled the contents from the bag. The hair cap was really interesting. I looked it over before putting my hair up into it and pulling it down around my hairline. It was filled with EEG electrodes.

Nurse Beauchemin turned around but didn't look directly at me yet. "I will connect you now."

He walked towards me with a bag full of white suction cups. My body tightened up and I had to remind myself to try and relax. Getting tense wouldn't change a thing. I just had to take these moments to chill as Nurse Beauchemin attached me to a number of quarter-sized white suction cups that were electronic sensors.

"While I understand you have signed away on liabilities via Senator Malone, I do have to reiterate that with the NeuroQuE there are additional risks such as, but not limited to, OBB or out-of-body experiences, feelings of disconnectedness, memory loss, brain death or even death. Do you understand?"

I couldn't bring myself to verbally agree to that because then it would feel too real. I just nodded, telling myself that *would not, could not* happen to me. On that awfully creepy note, I was instructed to return to the center of the room.

The wall opened up and I stood there like an alien stepping off a spaceship. I slowly walked towards the group with my arms pressed tight to my body. Nobody even reacted the way I felt they would have. I'm sure they could all tell this was uncomfortable for a teenage girl to basically be naked and center stage in front of an audience. It was like the most cliché nightmare ever was happening to me and it made my heart race. I couldn't stop scanning everyone's eyes to see if they were looking at me, judging me. They weren't. They were focused on their work and I was just highly sensitive data for the time being. Phew.

Richard ushered me onto a small round platform parallel to the NeuroQuE. Once on it, we were both elevated to the top. It was open and the water inside was perfectly flat and calm. He placed a plug over my nose and a mouthpiece into my mouth that connected via a tube so I could breathe.

"When I give you the cue, you will swing both legs over and insert them, then slide yourself in," he directed. "Don't resist, just let yourself submerge into the saline bath. It will simulate weightlessness. The water is a comfortable 98.7°. When you emerge, you will be yourself, but you will be confused. You won't know where you are. Now I am going to put these special goggles on over your eyes. They will be registering a range of activity, while also sending in messages. Do not take them off."

I closed my eyes and said a prayer because, in many ways, this was an act of faith. I didn't know what was about to happen next, and in a matter of moments, I would have absolutely no control.

Richard referred to his monitor. "Okay. All set for submergence in three, two, one…"

32

I RACED THROUGH memories of my time in Peru as my toes slipped into the NeuroQuE's lukewarm saline. Over and over, I recalled the memory of seeing my dad. My hope was that it would be one memory that I could retain in the reboot. In two seconds I was fully submerged. I was instantly transfixed by the serenity in the liquid's hollow silence. A meditative moment came over me as my mind and body felt at ease, but that floated away as moments always do. I was on the brink of having my brain tweaked and that was terrifying. I was unsure of my decision to do this. How could I get out of it now if I wanted to? *Should* I get out of this?

Streams of red, yellow and blue lights started to emit from the suction cups that were all over my body. The lights hit and rippled up and down the glass that enclosed me. I couldn't see beyond the glass, but I didn't need to. This showcase of lights was stunning. My whole self seemed to blend with the texture of the H20 and sodium chloride mixture and the movement of the lights. This suddenly felt absolutely right.

My body began to glide along in the water like it was being guided through a tunnel of lights. Before I had the chance to wonder what was happening, I was swiftly sucked down into a heap of nothingness. I couldn't see, hear or feel a thing. My mind was all that was left of me, but slowly, it, too, was being sucked away. The sensation was as if the second I had the beginning of a thought, it would be vacuumed into a funnel and squeezed tight into nothingness. Then there were no more thoughts. Only light.

Bright white light. Nothing but light.

Seconds became minutes became hours became days became years became free of time and on the continuum of the infinite. My being suddenly knew no bounds.

Bright white light.

Bright white light. I was hovering.

Bright white light. I soared at hyper speed.

Bright white light. I was far away from the life I knew.

Bright white light. I disconnected.

Bright white light. I connected to everything.

Bright white light. I took my last steps on the edge of time.

Bright white light forever and ever.

"Uhhh…" I moaned as I stirred awake from a deep sleep that felt like it lasted all winter.

I was underneath a muted, orange spotlight. My squinty eyes blinked to acclimate. One, two, I took a breath in and felt the air in my lungs spread into my veins and the blood streamed through my body. A tear trickled down from the corner of my eye. This life was miraculous and here I was in it.

But where was I? Had I passed out in the backpacking shop? My eyes had come to and I could now see that I was not where I was only moments ago. I was somewhere else. Panic entered my space. I looked at my hands. They were empty. Where was the eggplant backpack I was just holding? Where was the salesman that was just helping me decide between raincoats?

I lifted my head to a wave of vertigo and let it rest back down again. I turned my head to see the outlines of several people next to me. For some reason it took me a moment to gather my words, but I finally got them out. "Where am I? Who are you?"

A figure leaned in next to me. My vision came to and I saw her—

"Doro, it's me, Ellen."

"Ellen?!"

"Shh, yes, try and take it easy."

"How did you get here?"

I was beyond confused. Had she caught me here in Lima and brought me to the hub?

"Can you give us a moment?" Ellen asked several medical-looking people that surrounded us in the room.

I looked down at my body. Why was I under a sheet on an exam table?! I tried again to lift my head and I realized I was strapped down. My instincts made me squirm but I was definitely locked in hard.

A mature female doctor in an intricate black, robotic chair was looking at 3D holographic charts in the space in front of her. The whole contraption looked familiar— like Anika's BioNan mechanisms. It freaked me the heck out. Had they been messing with my implant?

"What is that? Who are they, Ellen? What is going on?! Let me off of this table!!!" I pleaded for dear life.

"Doro, if you calm down, I can explain."

The doctor stood up and approached Ellen Malone. "I understand that my team does not have clearance for the subject you wish to discuss with Ms. Campbell, but it's my obligation to provide reason for my concern."

"Please," Ellen suggested.

"The activity registering in Ms. Campbell's brain is highly unusual and I think it is imperative that we don't break from monitoring her."

"Why are they watching my brain?! Ellen!"

I started to heave. I was freezing yet my body broke into a sweat.

"Doro, you need to keep it together. Panicking won't help you," Ellen sternly warned me.

I was in no position to relax, though, and I just couldn't control my body from squirming.

Ellen turned back to the doctor. "Can you explain a little more?"

The doctor looked at me and then back to Ellen. The doctor was visibly disturbed by something she was watching on the monitor. "There are some erratic frequencies in her microtubules that we need to keep an eye on."

"Okay, I understand," Ellen said, "but I'm going to need twenty minutes with her right away, so unless it is a dire circumstance, I am going to have to ask you to give us this time."

"Alright then," the doctor replied reluctantly, then looked at me worriedly and back to the charts. "I will be watching your stats closely from the other room."

Ellen suggested to the doctor, "If you could, just wait in the wings on standby."

I wasn't sure that I wanted to be left completely alone with Ellen. Part of me believed I needed witnesses when I was incapacitated like this. It was times like these I could reflect upon the extreme value of autonomy.

The doctor agreed to Ellen's request. She and her team walked to the brick wall. It opened up for them. I watched them exit and the wall closed behind them. Ellen and I were alone. I was mad. I was confused. I wanted to be released from these cuffs.

"I'm going to unlock you now, Doro."

Without making a peep or a move, Ellen looked at the watch

on my wrists and ankles, and just like that they melted away. That was some crazy mastery of the flex implant. I jolted up to a seated position, and felt like I was going to faint. I braced myself on the table and started to shiver. It was suddenly freezing. I struggled to gather the sheet around my body. Ellen took her blazer off and tried to put it around me. I resisted her help and took it from her to do it myself. I pulled it over my shoulders. I had no words to say to her. She needed to be the one to do all the talking, and if she didn't have answers, then I was going to remain mute until someone told me *exactly* what was going on.

"I know this is incredibly bizarre, Doro."

I couldn't help but let out a nervous laugh.

"Last thing you knew, you were in Lima, Peru, and now suddenly you're here, with me, in a room with all this medical equipment and strange doctors. First let me tell you where you are. This is Claytor Lake's Center for Quantum Neurology and Consciousness Experimentations."

"What?!"

"You and I both knew that when this moment came along there would be nothing I could say to make you take my word, so we decided it would be best to let you tell yourself."

My eyes narrowed and I clenched my teeth together.

Ellen removed her flexer from her wrist and handed it to me. "Why don't you go ahead and put that on?"

In a way, this felt like she was extending an olive branch. A person's flexer is such a personal thing, and this one was tied directly to her implant. She really had to have faith in me to let me get my hands on this thing.

I took it and put it on.

"Retrieve FigureFlex video library," Ellen commanded.

A 3-D thumbnail library containing all of Ellen Malone's FigureFlex videos appeared hovering above Ellen's flexer on my wrist.

I looked up at her, slightly intrigued yet still skeptical. I looked back at the content library. One 3-D thumbnail was me in an outfit I didn't remember having ever worn.

"I don't understand." But I kind of did. It had appeared I recorded a FigureFlex of myself. But maybe they had created it to trick me, as if they had simulated it in a holographic computer program or something. I was no fool and I knew anything was possible here.

"You feel like you were at that outfitter in Peru moments, even seconds ago, but that was actually many days ago, and since then you have made a great many discoveries. The reason you feel it is still May 20th, is because we had to reboot your memory to that day through your Veil. Today is actually June 29th."

I started digging through my brain for any fragment of information to validate this, but I found nothing.

"That's... impossible."

"I know one thing you surely haven't forgotten is that in

Seneca nothing is impossible."

I eyed the 3-D hologram of myself and I noticed a scar on my arm— a scar that I didn't have before. That was puzzling. I slipped my hand under Ellen's blazer that I was wearing to feel that exact spot on my arm and was surprised to feel a healed scab where there was obviously a weeks old wound. I had no recollection of getting hurt.

"You recorded a message to yourself, to explain why you went through with this, and what you need to do next," Ellen said.

"How do I know it's real?"

Ellen smiled, "You asked the same question before you recorded it. *How will I know it's real when I watch it?* I'm going to leave you alone now, with yourself, and you can find out. Once I am out of the room you can press play."

"Okay."

Ellen left the room through the same wall that the doctors exited moments ago. I was alone now in this isolated chamber. My pale, clammy feet hung inches away from the stone floor. I shivered. In the silence I decided that, instead of seeking answers in my mind at this point, I would try to feel it in my gut. Should I press play? I stared eye to eye with the still of holographic me.

I slowly moved my finger to the play button and hovered over it for a moment before hitting it. The FigureFlex video began.

What's up, past but also present me? This is such a trip isn't it?

I was clearly in a much more chipper mood than I am now and it was obvious to me I wasn't under duress in the making of the video. *That*, I would have been able to tell.

Before I get into details, I just need to let myself be certain this is actually me and not some crazy S.O.I.L.-created, computer-simulated version of me, because we both know that would be the first thing we'd think.

I squinted. Ha. I know myself so well.

So here are a few facts: Killer will do anything for a marrow bone from Romeo's.

I laughed, and funnily enough this holographic-video-version of me paused for a beat for me to do so.

The ratio of two shots of espresso to one pump of mocha is the ultimate sweet spot.

"True"

Dave Grohl is a god.

I nodded emphatically, "Absolute fact."

I know you're agreeing with me right now and starting to enjoy this. We could go all day, but there is some very serious stuff to cover and the first, most important thing that I want you to know is that... Dad is alive.

I stood up from the exam table. I was eye to eye with myself and the heavy mask of doubt that covered me was crumbling. As I stared deep into the eyes of holographic me I could see the truth emanating from my soul. This was real. My dad was alive. I knew it. I knew he was.

Holographic me started to cry.

He's alive and he needs us.

Over the next fifteen minutes I listened as holographic me explained to current, yet past version of me, what my dad's involvement in Seneca was, the purpose of Doromium and what I needed to do to return to present me. I was in tears, but they had become tears of happiness.

Without a shadow of a doubt, I believed.

33

AFTER A SOLID six hours on that exam table, they couldn't seem to determine the reason for the erratic activity in my microtubules. I kept playing back the word "erratic." I felt particularly stable considering how weird this was— I wasn't the erratic one, this whole situation was erratic!

I watched Ellen grow impatient, quite out of character for her. She was progressively checking the time more often, taking deeper breaths and asking more and more questions. "Wouldn't we be aware if something calamitous was going to happen by now?" she asked.

The doctor, whom I came to know as Dr. Cairncross, had also grown more impatient, mostly with being questioned. Ellen and Dr. Cairncross stood on either side of me, discussing my well-being. "You're asking me to speculate. That is against my code of ethics," Dr. Cairncross quipped.

"I'm not suggesting unethical practice, but I need to assess her level of danger and measure it against the overall danger we face if we do not proceed immediately."

"I understand. Regardless, what you decide will be based upon assumptions."

Ellen put her hand on my shoulder. "Get up, Doro. It's time to get dressed."

"Senator Malone," the doctor interjected.

But Ellen was in fierce mode, standing tall and resolute. "Listen, I understand your concern and I am concerned, too, but all we can do is monitor the situation as we move forward. So whatever you need to do to make that happen, do it."

"Very well."

Dr. Cairncross headed back to her seat. Ellen motioned for me to get up and for one of the doctor's assistants to take me to let me get dressed again.

Several minutes later, Ellen and I left C-QNCE. Dr. Cairncross had equipped me with a device that would track my brain activity while I was off-site. She also dedicated her main physician's assistant to observing my chart twenty-four-seven and reporting to her on the hour.

Ellen and I took a private acoustic carrier to the computing center where Dom and I had completed Operation Crystal. I knew that the reason Ellen didn't say much to me was because of the bug, but she did brief me on Mars, the Departers and the Repairers.

Being here made me feel sad and nostalgic. This is where

Dom and I were when we first discovered the DNA of my father and it indicated his presence in the Colombian Seneca hub. It was during Operation Crystal that our love deepened. Dom and I were so distant now and it was my own fault for not telling him that he had been blamed for the flighter crash. I wondered if he was over me by now. The thought of that killed me. It had been so long since I left for Peru to find my dad. I wished I knew more details of that meeting with my dad. But I realized that the sooner I could complete this task, discover the perpetrator on my flex implant and pave the way for Ellen and Gilroy to uncover their motivation, the quicker I could get back to my actual, current self and those memories.

I hoped with all my heart that I would also still have a chance with Dom. There could never be a love like that again and I imagined that when we revived it, it would be more powerful than ever. On that note, I turned my attention to the joystick.

First things first, I pulled all my current data to the FlexOculi screen in front of me. Once it was up, I pinpointed my implant's incoming and outgoing signals. In a normal functioning implant the signal would just be coming in and going out of my brain to spots I had determined. In this case, it was sending and receiving to a remote location. The message pathway was clear. For now. Still, I had to find out where it was coming from, so I would send a message out and track its path.

This kind of code breaking was normally a cakewalk, but for

some reason I hit a brick wall this time. Or, more like a signal wall that tried to bounce the signal back to me like a mirror instead of allowing it to complete its one-way path.

I fidgeted in my seat and squeezed my fists together. Ellen noticed I was becoming irritated.

"What's up?"

"Nothing. Just a little hiccup." I closed my eyes and tried to extinguish my frustration. Frustration would only stimulate the part of my brain that obstructed my problem solving capabilities. It always did, but the older I got, the better I got at dealing with it by acknowledging it and getting it under wraps.

I remembered back to when I had broken a code in Eastern Europe that held the gaming algorithm I piggybacked for my poker account. It felt like another lifetime even though it was less than two years ago that I had broken the world's biggest gaming algorithms and funneled the money to an offshore account. I was fifteen and pulling in millions, but was too naive to cover my tracks. This was going to be different.

The coding here on the source location of this bug looked awfully familiar to the gaming defenses, just a bit more advanced. So I tapped into my Veil and copied some of the formulas from the gaming algorithms, brought them over, tweaked them and ran my coding again.

Wait. I eyed the messages that flew back at me.

This was different. Someone was on the other end, waiting for me.

I was suddenly inundated with communication from dozens of sources, each one completely different than the other. The messages made no sense though and I couldn't locate the original signal. Someone was clearly firing them off with the intention of distracting me and keeping me from the actual source. I could play that game, too, but I knew I had to come correct with an even heavier handed game than they had. I had to shift into offense now and put them on their toes.

My move was to create a mirror on my end and lure in the barrage of communication again, to which I would attach a virus and they would all bounce back and forth from my mirror to theirs, multiplying exponentially so that the coder on that end could never kill my virus. For every virus they quarantined, three more would be created.

Theirs would be no easy feat, because I wrote my virus to morph attributes on each bounce, and I wrote the coding so that every time it bounced back to me, my immunity blocked it out. The coder on the other end was consumed with defending its systems against my virus attack, and this rendered them incapable of sending new messages from any new alias locations.

While I had them in a coding freeze they would not be able to get out of, I jumped each mirror and followed the digital line of communication to the end of its road. Twenty messages fired off in all sorts of crazy directions, only to end up in one place: somewhere in southeast Asia where anonymous data hubs are set up in entire data cities. But there was no way this sophisticated hacking was just someone across the world having fun with me. Behind one of these mirrors was the true location that had created all the alias locations to try and disorient me.

Here they came exactly how I wanted them, trying to play my game, sending a virus at me, but little did they know, I had set up a virus receptor to quarantine, descramble and reveal its origination. I did just that and on my thirty third mirror jump I found the one unique location.

I traced the source of the virus to map coordinates, and the map coordinates were identical to that of the bug.

"Got it."

Ellen breathed a huge sigh of relief. "You're incredible," she said, and patted me on the shoulder.

I'm not going to lie. It felt great to make Ellen proud.

"So where is it coming from?" she asked.

"Well, these are the coordinates," I said, and opened up the projection of my FlexOculi for Ellen to see the image that was in front of me:

39°00'12.8"N 77°26'29.4"W

She then opened up the projection from her FlexOculi so that I could see as she input the coordinates. The FlexMap graphic popped up and zoomed to the point where the signal being sent to and from my implant was originating— a location in the Aboves: Ashburn, Virginia.

"No kidding," Ellen muttered under her breath.

"What, Ellen, what is it?"

"Flex Technology Corporation," she said.

I didn't get it. "Why would Flex Technology Corporation want to interfere with me going to find my dad?"

Ellen's eyes shifted from left to right, back and forth, but she wasn't actually looking at anything. She was inside her head trying to figure this out, her mouth slightly open in amazement. It was cool to watch her process her thoughts. Normally she had already completed her thought processes by the time she spoke to me.

The pieces of the puzzle were coming together.

"Listen," Ellen said as she stood. "We need to get you back into residence and you are going to continue with session as usual, as if absolutely nothing has changed."

"Ellen, you know I respect you, but I'm not continuing with any 'plan' until you make sense of this for me."

I wasn't taking any half truths right now. I saw her thinking and I wanted in on that. I deserved in on that.

"I know you want answers. I do, too," she said. "But we can't call attention to this, any of this. There is a war going on that is bigger than us, and we need to quietly uncover all the information and the players."

"Why is Flex Technology Corporation in my head, Ellen?"

Ellen sat back. She looked me in my eye. She put her hands on her knees.

"Doro, Flex Technology is the main financier behind The Seneca Society. They were the only ones with the money and technology to build this underground society, but here is the thing. Flex Tech is new money and they have a whole lot of it. Practically too much to count and they want to keep it right here on Earth, so they built Seneca to test this model society and perfect the use of Doromium. The only way it could have been approved to do all of this was by the old money, the powerful families that have been around for hundreds of years. As you know, many of those are Departers like the Wallingsfords. The Departers have a different endgame in mind. Both sides realize that knowledge is power, and Doromium is the very piece that it all hinges on. I honestly believed we would have traced the bug back to a specific Departer source, but the fact that this is a Repairer offense changes everything. I believe Flex Corp. was preemptively blocking you from contact with your dad because the Departers were close to using that relationship to their advantage."

"My relationship with my dad? How could they possibly do that?"

"You are the next generation to take your dad's legacy. You can influence him like nobody else can, so your identifying with

Departers or Repairers is crucial to their agendas."

I understood what was happening. There was a battle for mind control. It wasn't between me and another party. It was between two dueling factions, over my mind as a means to control over everyone. Unless I had all my memories intact and my mind in its optimal state, I would just continue to be a pawn in someone else's game.

"I need to go get my memories back."

"I know you do. Problem is, Dr. Cairncross can't put you back in the NeuroQuE until the erratic activity ceases."

"What?! How do we know when that will be?"

"We don't."

"Ellen, come on, that's crazy. I can't just go back to business as usual with this outdated frame of mind."

"It's way too dangerous. The risks are heightened in your current state."

"I don't care! I can't stay like this with a bug on my implant and no memories of the past month! No way. I can't just accept going on with this level of vulnerability."

"I know and I agree. But it is all a matter of timing. We need to play the game right. I was sent to Hub 48 to reprimand you and bring you back, and I did that. They think we're their pawns and that they've got us exactly where they want us. Now you just need to carry on as if you're angry you didn't find your dad and accepting that you were wrong. Dr. Cairncross is monitoring your neurological processes and as soon as things even out, we will return to Claytor Lake."

I didn't like it one bit, but I got it. I would bite my tongue and slide back to session in the morning like I was just another ordinary scholar harvesting my potential in the futuristic land of opportunity.

34

THERE WAS AN incredibly strange tingling in my veins as I headed into S.E.R.C., knowing I would come face-to-face with Dom and Reba. I was so let down and upset with them both since they had basically ditched me to let me set out for South America on my own. My heart hurt, my stomach turned, and I had a bit of a migraine coming on. It was the perfect brew of sadness, lack of sleep and *erratic* brain activity.

After two sleepless nights plagued by increasing confusion, I made a decision early this morning that, when I got home from sessions later in the day, I would begin the manual process to restore my memories. It would require countless hours of sifting through the back-up in my Veil to scrub and reinstall memories from my time in South America.

In the meantime, I would avoid the guys. I couldn't keep track of what was past and what was present and conversing with them would only add fuel to the fire of confusion.

"Campbella, I didn't think I'd see you back here so soon."

"Huh?"

I spun around to see Reba, with a gentle smile on his face, but definitely not rocking his normal level of spunk. I had to think quick. Avoidance was off the table now, for Reba at least. "Yeah, um, it didn't work out... the trip."

"I see."

I wanted so badly to remain in sweet Reba's company, but at the same time I had to get away from him before this conversation got sticky. It would be any moment that he would start tapping into how I was really feeling, and I just couldn't go down that path and subsequently have to lie to him. He'd know I was lying. Oh, man, what a slippery slope. The pit of my stomach squeezed and gurgled.

Just as I was fumbling through a concoction of an excuse for bailing on this conversation, I spotted Dom about fifty yards down. At the same time that I saw him, he saw me. We had two completely different reactions. He lit up. I froze. But why was he so happy to see me when all I could replay in my mind was him being so angry at Ty's Sushi before I left for Peru? I didn't know how to respond.

"I gotta go," I said to Reba. "I'm sorry."

"Wait, we still have time before session. Oh, look, there's Dom!"

I couldn't formulate a complete thought on what I should do. I just felt slammed against the wall and I needed to get out of there.

"Dom!" Reba called out, "Look who's back!"

Dom came running towards me, and instead of being excited and happy, I was anxious and confused. I literally froze against the wall and plastered my hands against it as it was the only thing solid in my space.

"Doro!"

Dom lifted me into a huge hug and spun me around.

"When did you get back?! Why didn't you flex me?"

Dom's eyes studied my face as we were still in an embrace. He looked as though he was about to kiss me, but then he stopped and noticed my confused expression that I just couldn't hide no matter how hard I tried. I couldn't bear the way this all felt inside, everything so out of sync and inconsistent with the reality that I understood. Dom's presence wasn't comforting me and I didn't know what to do with my unease other than jet.

"Guys, I'm sorry. I have to go talk to Professor Shields about some past due report. Catch up later?"

Dom took a step back and peered at me with a furrowed brow. Reba's eyes darted from Dom to me. Reba was piecing it together. I wanted him to stop.

"I'm sorry," I said before spinning around and bolting down the golden hall. I felt both sets of the guys' eyes glued to me, but I didn't look back. It felt wrong, but I'd just have to right this later. My head hung low and I held my hand over my stomach that growled in turmoil as if it had a mind of its own, one that was at odds with the one in my head.

I peeled around the corner into my Seneca civics and ethics session as if it was a safe hiding place. Professor Shields was surprised and delighted to see me, and I, too, was relieved to be back in that room. This session space felt totally normal, like a memory that had not changed and, therefore, it was very comforting and safe. I needed that.

"Campbell! I'm so glad to see you're okay!"

"I am," I stated somewhat inquisitively. "Why wouldn't I be okay?"

"I just thought you went through a lot last month, but it's excellent that you're back. We have a huge FigureFlex trip to the Aboves today. I'm glad you won't miss it."

My armor peeled back for a moment and my naked self peered out from behind it. What did he know and why did he know it? I had to know.

"Why would I have missed it?" I asked.

"Oh, I just wasn't sure how long it would take to recover from your aneurysm. I understand it was pretty serious. But I know you're a tough kid with a mind of steel, so I'm not surprised you've bounced back."

"Thanks." I quipped. An *aneurysm*— quite the cover. I smirked inside, imagining Ellen sending out this fake information.

"They said you might have a tough time and I should take it easy on you in session, so you just let me know if any of it feels too heavy and, if it does, we can FigureFlex you back to the classroom to review some past material."

"Okay. I should be fine, but I'll let you know if I don't feel good."

"Wonderful."

I spotted Jennifer Wallingsford at a desk taking notes on her FlexPad. She looked up at me as I took a seat at the desk next to her. "Welcome back," she said with her trademark posture and confident, welcoming gaze.

"Hi, thanks, Jennifer."

Jennifer and I were stopped short of conversing as the bell rang and Professor Shields gave us the introduction for our FigureFlex trip into the Aboves. Along with my eighteen civics & ethics sessionmates, we headed up for a tour of three locations in North America that had been severely stricken by environmental devastation as a result of a deteriorating atmosphere and pervasive pollution.

First we glided through the swampland that had once been Louisiana. It was less than a decade ago that people actually lived in this state, but now the only sign of life was toxic algae that grew in the water and spread like disease. If we were actually, physically there, we would be exposed to all sorts of potential sickness and disease. Second, we went to Alaska where the last of the mighty glaciers had thawed. We learned that this had created a heck of another gold rush as all the miners have been fighting over land that was covered in ice for thousands of years. We saw with our own eyes make-shift tent communities of men that had posted up there to battle it out for the riches. It had even become a draw for people from other professions that had derailed in the past decade, like retailers and farmers. It was really something that gold, the oldest standard in monetary value, had retained its value amidst all the digital currencies across the globe.

Our last stop was in the Midwest, a place I had never been. But it was close to where my dad was from in Wisconsin. We climbed the steps to the top of a mill that looked out to hundreds of miles of deserted farmland.

"As you can see," Professor Shields pointed out, "a lot has changed since we have been underground. These were once working farms, full of Holsteins that provided a huge portion of the country with dairy products, corn, soy, you name it. Don't be blinded by the fact that in Seneca we have the best of the best of everything. We should all practice gratitude daily for that. Here in the Aboves the broken food supply had so many repercussions. Too many to list off, but as you can imagine, farmers have lost their livelihoods, and entire ecosystems have failed, globally. Water is tainted with acid, the plants can't grow, and consequently there is no pollen for the bees whose colonies are in a state of collapse. Ladies and Gentlemen, you are all smart enough to understand the domino effect here... and just how widespread this deterioration of life on our planet has spread and will spread, like wild fire."

Professor Shields wanted us to have our own time to absorb the details of this landscape, and that we did. We looked out over the tortured land. It was such a contrast to the sparkling golden halls I had become accustomed to. I found it heartbreaking how life could change in a flash. I wished I could experience a normal life in the Aboves with Dom, that we could go to a normal school, run along the beach in Santa Monica and grab an ice cream out in the sunshine. I knew that would never happen and it was a crushing realization.

Jennifer and I caught up as we walked down the steps from the mill.

"What's wrong?" Jennifer inquired.

I rubbed the stone on the necklace I had on as we pensively walked along through the deserted Holstein farm. I didn't remember where it came from, but it felt good. "I was just thinking of Dom... my ex. Feels so wrong to say."

"Aw, well, you have remnants of feelings for him, that's understandable. But don't worry, you will be over him soon. Just remember, you have to stay focused on yourself. You have too much to accomplish to let boys like that mess you up."

In a way she was right. But was Dom actually trying to mess

me up, or did we have a miscommunication? This FigureFlex tour was eye-opening, but what I really needed was some mind-opening and that wouldn't happen until I was back in my residence, alone with my Veil, refilling my shallow database of lost memories.

35

It was a long first day back in S.E.R.C. By the time I got home I could barely keep my eyes open, but there was no way I would let myself get any shuteye when there was outstanding information just waiting to be mined from the archives of my Veil. I downed a quad shot mocha that I picked up on the way home because I knew it would take double my normal dose of espresso to get the job done.

I carefully pulled a Beatles record from its near mint-condition jacket that was almost a century old. It was one of my favorites to listen to with my dad when he was doing his work, and now it was time to get on with mine.

Just as my Veil erected in the space in front of my face by way of my FlexOculi, these lyrics hit:

Your outside is in and your inside is out.

No matter what lyrics came next, I just keep repeating those ones over and over in my head.

Your outside is in and your inside is out.

The back-up took up an insane amount of space and it was daunting to imagine the amount of time that it would take to get through the whole thing, so I began by telling myself that I would take it in chunks: one step at a time.

It didn't help that an underlying heartache permeated my thoughts no matter what I did. I was so disconnected from everyone— Dom, my mom, Reba, and I had completely lost all my friendships back home when I left for Seneca. All I had that remained with my friends in the Aboves were remnants of each other in our hearts. It was so painful at first that I actually had to block it out. I couldn't bear going through something like that again. A hole expanded inside of my chest. I wondered if any of my loved ones thought of me, too. This loneliness could kill me before any neurological procedure could. I could easily have curled up in a ball to sob those feelings out until I had no tears left to cry, but I had to push my feelings down for now. I had to get to work to restore the memories that would help me understand where I was and where I was going next.

I could play the memories back in the sequential order in which they had occurred before I reinserted them into my permanent mind, but they wouldn't stick unless I issued that command. I had to deconstruct the encoding inside the neural pathways that constructed each individual memory to make sure they were clear or washed free of the bug before I reinserted it for good.

Performing a wash on each memory would be an incredibly time-consuming task, so what I decided to do was keep only the ones that were clearly pertinent to the situation at hand.

I took my mind back to Peru and found the first memory I had on the day of that May 20th back-up when I was at the outfitter. The exact moment that the bug hit me was when I held up the eggplant colored backpack. I wanted to remember that, so I scrubbed the memory and reinserted it.

Immediately after that process, I felt the floor move beneath my feet and I braced myself for a bout of dizziness. I closed my eyes until the spins stopped. Then I took a drink of water and a few deep breaths. My palms were sweaty from all the caffeine and I was uncomfortably jittery, too, but I needed to channel that into focus rather than let it destroy me.

There were no other memories of value from inside the outfitter so I moved on. Along I jogged through my journey on the bus, and out into the woods where it became insanely convoluted. This section of my memories didn't even make sense — they felt more like hallucinations that some other person had. Had I fallen against the cliff in the pouring down rain? I referred back to my scar and touched it. I closed my eyes. I couldn't remember. But the scar on my body indicated it *did* happen. I had to dig deeper into these stored memories, but it just didn't feel real. I hated that I couldn't piece together and make sense of it. I played back that memory again and tried to feel myself fall. I needed to keep it, whether it was real or not, because it was the only thing that could explain this weeks-old gash on my arm.

I suddenly had a dizzy spell even worse than the last one. I dropped my head into my hands. It took almost double the time for the vertigo to pass, and when it did, I felt extra parched. I stood up to go get more water, but I lost my footing and had to sit back on the bed with my heavy head in my hands. Come on, Doro, this is important! Don't fail yourself now just because you can't handle a little discomfort.

I lifted my head from the cradle of my hands and peered at the clock through squinted eyes— five in the morning! How was that possible?! Were the intense NeuroQuE procedure and erratic brain activity responsible for this impeding state of delirium? Or was it the fact that I hadn't a full night of rest in God knows how long? R.E.M. was just a dream for this girl. I didn't have dreams anymore. My subconscious was lost. Nights were a blur of fading off and startling awake into accelerated thoughts that wouldn't stop. The nocturnal mayhem produced pools of sweat into which my sanity fell and swam away.

I opened my eyes but couldn't see straight and when I closed them again, it was like I got whisked away in a gust of wind. I reached back for the ground that moved farther away. Forgotten days blended together into a tornado of sensations and sounds that made no sense. I tried to make it stop so I could recall what I'd experienced in the past few weeks, or months, but it felt like a vacuum had sucked me down from the sky into a pit of raging tumbleweeds. I was sprawled out on the edge of a body of water but I couldn't drink. I couldn't move…

But I wasn't dead so I wasn't going to stop. I couldn't stop. I was getting closer to the memories that I needed to retrieve.

The winds picked up and I tumbled again. Harder this time. But in the cyclone of sounds— computerized beeps and swooshes and howling winds— I heard their voices: Dom and Reba. They echoed in the darkness and then there was rain, crashing down. It was inside me and it was outside me. My clothes were sopping wet. Steam came off of my body and encircled Dom and Reba, there in the wilderness… and Ellen! They were all there, and then they were gone.

I stopped. I planted my hands and knees into the gooey muck. Or was it my bed? It was both. I needed to plant this memory back in my mind immediately so I could feel right about my friends.

I played the memory back again.

Dom and Reba tried to get through to me on FigureFlex. I was in the wilderness. I saw myself from above.

"He came for me," I muttered to myself. There was calm in the chaos. I felt his energy radiating into my heart. But the calm proved elusive and I couldn't fend off the intensifying shakes. My disequilibrium cranked up tenfold as I took that memory back in.

I couldn't see straight even if I tried. I couldn't open my eyes to look at the files I needed to pull because my vision shook and electricity zapped away at my brain, frying it like a chicken nugget.

I had to keep going. I forced my eyes open. I was on my bed. I tried again to access more memories.

Nausea bubbled from the pit of my stomach up through my throat and I dry heaved.

Ring. Ring. Ring.

I stirred awake. I was curled up in a tight ball on my bed and quickly shot up to a seat. I gasped for a breath. I moaned and rubbed at my temples. A throbbing headache paralyzed me.

Ring. Ring. Ring.

Someone was frantic at my door.

I stood up, dizzy like crazy, and thrust my arms out for balance. I flexed through the door speaker, "Who is it?"

A voice amplified back through, "Doro, it's Mom. Please open your door!"

I immediately commanded the door to open.

She rushed in and threw her arms around me.

"Oh my god, Doro."

"What?"

"Thank god you're okay."

My mom burst into tears. "You've got to stop doing this," she sobbed.

"Huh? What's wrong?"

I felt so confused, and I just wanted to hug my mom back, but I had to sit.

"Doro. Honey…"

My mom sat down next to me and hugged me tight.

"You've got me worried sick."

"What happened?"

"Really, Doro? For starters, you just returned from being missing with no word for almost a month, and now I haven't heard from you in days. I thought you were just upset with me but then I got a call from one of your session leaders looking for you since you haven't shown up for two days."

"What time is it?"

I looked at my clock: it was six o'clock, two days after I went on the FigureFlex tour of the Aboves. Insane. I hadn't slept for that long of a stretch in my entire life. Not ever.

"Is this related to our argument the other day?" my mom quietly asked.

"What argument?"

I looked at her sad eyes. She didn't have on any make-up and she had obviously been crying. Her eyes were bloodshot. Her hair was down and it looked more gray than ever.

"Doro, you're really scaring me."

It destroyed me once again that I had done this to her. I was killing my mom and I didn't mean for that at all. All I wanted was for her to be happy.

"Mom, it's okay. I'm fine. I was just wiped out from all this work I've been doing."

"This is crazy. *All this work!* You're still a kid, Doro. You need a break, and I am going to demand it."

"No!" Ahh! My head was killing me. It felt like it was being wrung like a wet rag.

"We need to call a doctor."

"Mom. No. Please. I promise I will rest. I just need a little bit of time. I promise you. Please."

"Honey."

"If I can just get another full night's sleep. I promise, okay? I will be more conscientious about getting rest. Mom, please."

I could tell how hard it was for my mom to let me guide what happened next. It was the nurse and mother in her that wanted to take care of me and prescribe a doctor's visit. But she didn't know what I really needed, and oh man, if she knew even a fraction of what I had been through since coming to Seneca, it would give her a massive heart attack.

She rubbed my back and, for the first time in as long as I could remember, comfort washed over me. I breathed a huge sigh of relief and that put a little smile on my mom's face. I closed my eyes and faded.

36

MY MOM STAYED with me through the weekend, waking me up to eat and drink and periodically wiping my forehead with a cool cloth. The symptoms I had were unlike anything I'd ever felt. It was like a mental flu had taken hold of my whole body sending shockwaves from my fingers to my toes and leaving a brassy taste in my mouth no matter how I tried to cover it up. My mom, the best nurse in the history of the world (inspired by her hero Clara Barton, founder of the American Red Cross,) said she'd never seen anything like it. She said that my body was probably recovering from whatever trauma I'd been through over the past month. I maintained that I couldn't recollect a thing.

I couldn't wait to move on with the motions of going to session so I could come back and pull more memories. I still needed to get up to speed on my status with Dom and understand the full picture with my dad.

Monday morning I was headed back to S.E.R.C., and my mom was headed back to pick up Killer from the doggy play center he had spent many days in now. She'd probably have to nurse him back to normal, because he was always wiped out after doggy day care in the Aboves. Killer seriously loved being with other dogs. He went bananas for girl dogs. I missed my bouncy furball and looked forward to snuggling him again, bad breath and all. My mom made me promise to flex her my whereabouts after session.

As I stepped off the acoustic carrier, my head started to pound again, but it actually wasn't as bad as it had been right after I had reinserted my memories. I figured if anything was terribly wrong, Dr. Cairncross would make sure I was called back to Claytor Lake.

I saw Reba down the golden hall. He smiled when he saw me and started heading my way. Just then I felt someone take my hand.

"Dorothy."

"Jennifer, hi."

"I haven't seen you around. Are you okay?" she inquired, appearing quite concerned with a furrowed brow and eyes locked on mine.

"Yeah, I just had a little bug."

"Oh no. Well, listen. I hope you're up for a little adventure because I'd like for you to accompany me to the Aboves. In real life, not via FigureFlex."

"Really, *me*, why? What's going on?"

I noticed Reba had stopped short of us and was watching our conversation.

"It's a surprise, but I will say, it is a *huge* deal."

"I don't have clearance to traverse though."

"When you're with me, you have clearance for anything."

I could not deny that I was intrigued. I looked over and smiled and waved at Reba. He had an intriguing look about him. Squinted eyes and a stoic face. Like he was unsure about Jennifer and I conversing and trying to make emotional calculations about it.

"You know, thanks, but I shouldn't go," I said.

Jennifer was visibly surprised that I turned down the offer.

"I think you're making a mistake," she said. "My dad has some big plans for us."

Us, I thought. Wow. This trip to the Aboves was no minor offer. What could these plans possibly be? "Plans for *us*? Like what?"

"Don't you think you should at least come give it a listen?"

As far as I knew, Frank Wallingsford was one of the most powerful people in Seneca. He was a guy who believed in me, and basically saved Dom and me in that Seneca Senate hearing where Gregory tried to have us banished to the Aboves. Plus, he had given me the opportunity to stay in Seneca in the first place, and he'd never done anything to betray me. The least I could do was see what was on the table. I couldn't trust his brother, Billy, with all his power company wheelings and dealings, but he was not his brother.

I looked back to Reba. He was deadpan. I shrugged, not sure why he didn't just come up to talk with us. I was too curious to walk away and not know what these proposed plans were.

Jennifer and I took an acoustic carrier to the ascension dome where we were joined by two men in black. They escorted us up to the fairytale Great Falls grass and there was an awaiting flighter for the four of us.

Once we were in flight, I inquired some more about our destination. "I have to say the suspense is killing me."

Jennifer's face brightened. "It will be worth it. I don't know why we don't hang out more, but I think we are going to get to see more of each other."

I was familiar with this flight path. We were headed back into Washington, D.C., on the tail end of morning traffic.

"Well, I'm not sure exactly what I did to deserve the trip, but thanks for bringing me along."

"Of course! Are you kidding? It's our pleasure to have you. Actually, my dad suggested you come. Like I said, he's got big plans for us."

Now I was on the edge of my seat. Especially because each time I had a big meeting with Frank Wallingsford, my life shifted in a major way.

"Can you give me a hint?"

"Sure." Jennifer smiled. "Have you ever thought of yourself as a pioneer?"

"Not exactly."

"Well, you should."

"Only if I get a horse and a covered wagon."

The Wallingsfords had some grandiose, notorious reputations, but they had always been awesome to me. Frank Wallingsford was the one who had invited me to stay in Seneca to begin with. He was also responsible for demoting Gregory Zaffron and for initiating Operation Crystal. I wanted to stay on the up and up with them, and I knew they had the power to help bring my family back together. I also felt it would be advantageous to solidify my alignment with them while Ellen was busy uncovering the backstory with Flexer Technology Corporation's placing a bug on my implant.

"I have no idea what that means but I'm totally up for pioneering with you."

"Good," Jennifer said, and she pointed out the window. "I love this building."

We landed at the base of the steps for The Smithsonian's National Air and Space Museum, put on our protective goggles, and stepped out onto a striped white crosswalk. Today it was secured off from the public, and there were several hundred protesters outside.

"What's that all about?" I asked.

"There are always people that will fight change even if that change is good for them," Jennifer said. "Know what I mean?"

I did.

Jennifer and I were accompanied inside the museum by the men in black. It was a gorgeous space that we entered, flooded with natural light through the wall of windows. Even though the artificial sunlight in Seneca was a darn good replicate, nothing could beat the real thing. I looked up at the soaring ceilings lined in geometrical white truss.

The buzz and energy inside were infectious. Powerful people mingled and made their way in the same direction as Jennifer and I.

"This was always my favorite museum as a kid," Jennifer told me.

"I can see why."

"Ever had astronaut ice cream?" she asked.

I smiled. "No, but it sounds amazing."

Jennifer instructed our escorts that we'd make a pit stop in the gift shop, where she bought me a vacuum-sealed pack of Neapolitan ice cream— chocolate, vanilla, strawberry. I immediately opened it, and nibbled on it as we walked into the Milestones of Flight Hall.

"What do you think?" she asked.

"Interesting." It was really chalky.

Jennifer laughed. "Right? Well you'd better get used to it."

Get used to it? Was Jennifer implying that I'd be going into space with her? I needed be careful with how I responded. I just wished my lingering headache would go away. Power through, Doro. Power through. This was huge.

The Milestones of Flight Hall was incredible with various aircrafts of yesteryear suspended in the air above us. In the air between a spaceship and a podium on a stage a digital 3D projection read: *Southern Gate Exploration Welcomes You to Mars*. Time lapse images of people building out agricultural and city infrastructure on the red planet played with inspirational piano music.

I was pretty blown away and couldn't take my eyes off the projection as we made our way to the first row directly in front of the podium. Was the stuff on the projection actually happening in real time, or was this a simulation of what they'd like to happen in the future? I wondered.

There was a positive buzz in the air with a pretty diverse cross-section of people mingling at their seats. Some I recognized from the Seneca Senate when we had the debate. Then I saw Ellen. Of course Ellen was here. But why wasn't she out sorting the Flexer Technology Corporation issue? We caught one another's gaze, but suddenly a hush came over the crowd and I saw a man in a suit had taken to the podium.

"Ladies and Gentlemen, if you would all take your seats," the man requested over the loudspeaker.

I was already seated next to Jennifer, who was next to her brother, G.W., who was next to their Uncle Billy. The seat beside me was empty, but Brittany came up with Senator Gilroy, her mother and sister.

"Hi, Brittany!"

"Doro!"

We gave each other a huge hug.

Senator Gilroy gave a little nod and smile.

"So cool to see you here," I said to Brittany.

"I didn't know you were back." Brittany looked over my shoulder. "Hi, Jennifer."

"Hi, Brittany."

I sensed a palpable tension between the two. Senator Gilroy and his wife walked past me to shake hands with each Wallingsford before taking their seats.

Brittany and I sat down. "Let's catch up after this," I said to her.

She nodded. "We can go for a ride if you want."

"I'd love that."

I turned to Jennifer. She smiled and looked away, up to the podium where the man cleared his throat and then spoke into the microphone.

"Esteemed members of Congress, Mr. President, Mr. Vice-President, NASA, Southern Gate Electric Corporation and guests. Welcome."

The crowd cheered. Everyone was thrilled to be here.

My head felt pretty heavy and the pounding didn't cease between my eyes, but, if anything, the energy here helped. I was really starting to feel excited that I was included in what felt like such a momentous occasion. The last time I was in a room with a few of these people I was being highly scrutinized, and now I was with them, like an apprentice future leader of the world, and it felt incredible. I just needed to get my head back to normal so I could fully engage in this.

The man spoke up as the applause subsided, "For those of you whom I don't have the pleasure of knowing, I am Rupert Neville, the Director of the Air and Space Museum. I want to thank you all for being here with us today. It is my great honor and privilege to give you a man who truly needs no introduction, for it is his passion and perseverance that have brought us all here today, and for that we are all tremendously grateful."

I looked at Jennifer and G.W. They were beaming. I felt this way about my dad. I was happy for them but a bit jealous, too.

"Ladies and Gentlemen, our very own United States Congressman Frank Wallingsford!"

Without hesitation the entire room rose for a standing ovation as Wallingsford made his way to the podium with both of his hands up waving to everyone and a gigantic smile on his face.

"Thank you! Thank *you*! Thank *YOU*!"

More cheers.

I found that I was clapping more than usual, as if this was a concert or something. It just felt big, whatever it was...

"301 million miles away we are making a new home. Today is one of the most exciting days of my life because I get to share this with all of you, and *we* get to share this with the world! The advances we have made towards absolute peace and prosperity are astounding. The departure is upon us, Ladies and Gents. *This is our future!*"

Everyone cheered again. It was as though every time Wallingsford opened his mouth the cheers got louder.

He pointed up to the projection. "See that?! *That,* my friends, is progress. That is what President John F. Kennedy was talking about in 1962 when he said, *'This country of the United States was not built by those who waited and rested and wished to look behind them. This country was conquered by those who moved forward— and so will space.'* Indeed, it is one of the greatest tragedies known to mankind that we need to leave our precious Earth, but *we,* my friends, we will prevail because we are moving forward to live in space! This is no longer a dream. This is our reality. With our stronghold of science, knowledge and information we are moving into an era of a brand-new life in space. We are now welcoming volunteers to depart every two months for a prosperous existence on Mars. These pioneers will be setting up our new home for us and this has all been made possible by two organizations. Today I want to thank the

National Aeronautics and Space Administration for their work in exploring our extraordinary universe and handing us access to all that they have uncovered over the years. They are putting their knowledge in great hands with our country's leading developer in technology and science infrastructure, our very own Southern Gate Exploration. Please join me in welcoming the dashingly intelligent, but not-quite-as-handsome-as his brother, CEO of Southern Gate Exploration, Billy Wallingsford."

The room erupted in cheers.

Wow. Hearing this with a crowd made it feel monumental. NASA was handing the reins for Mars' exploration over to SGE Corp. I also recognized that the messaging here, no matter how promising, was heavy-handed Departer propaganda. Everyone was susceptible to it, myself included.

Billy Wallingsford stood up from beside G.W. and waved to the adoring crowd before making his way to the podium to hug his brother Frank Wallingsford, and then he stepped to the microphone as Frank took a step back.

"Thank you for such a warm welcome, and for humoring my little brother. This is such an exciting time. What my brother said could not be more true. Our ancestors looked to the night sky, catalogued the stars and made up great stories of the heavens. Our forefathers searched the heavenly bodies, developed mathematics to describe the motion of the planetary bodies and sent probes into space to make new discoveries. And can you believe it? Now we are right at the forefront, riding the wave they sent to us! We are honored to be in the position to make it possible for all women, men, and children in the world to have a choice to leave our planet and go to Mars to continue the pioneering that our forefathers have done for millennia. We'd love for you to join us today in visiting some of our informational centers here to learn about the advances we are making and how you can contribute. Let's not ever forget that it is a collective effort that has made, and will continue to make, this all possible! This is a great day for all Americans and all of the world. My thanks to NASA for bestowing this honor upon us by passing the torch to allow SGE to usher in a new era of the good life on the red planet! In closing, I'm going to piggyback off my brother today by quoting President John F. Kennedy. '*As we set sail we ask God's blessing on the most hazardous and dangerous and greatest adventure on which man has ever embarked.*'"

"Thank you and God bless you all!" Billy trumpeted, and the room went wild.

37

THAT EPIC SPEECH left me questioning my stance. Before today I was anti-Departer, pro-Repairer. Seeing all this imagery, though, and believing in the potential of space exploration, I couldn't help but imagine that I, along with my family, could very well be one of the pioneers on Mars. Becoming versed in backstory of both the Departers and Repairers allowed me the recognition of the strong sentiments on both sides, and gave me the fortitude to form my own opinions. I didn't want to be manipulated one way or the other by rhetoric.

The whole audience shuffled to another part of the Air and Space Museum where a gala was set up with a banquet. I was starving so I beelined it for the food as Jennifer got pulled in to talk with some of her parents' friends.

There was a kids' table that offered grilled cheese with the crust cut off. That had my name all over it. I saw G.W. spot me enjoying my first bite. He snuck away from the group he'd been mingling with to join me at the kids' table. "Grilled cheese is my favorite!" he proclaimed.

"I love it!" I said. "I am so grateful for your family bringing me along," I gushed.

"Ah, we love you, Doro! You're so awesome."

"Aw, thanks! But I haven't done anything that awesome, have I?"

"You're just more down to earth than the people I am used to, and I appreciate that. You're the real deal!"

Brittany walked up. G.W. put his arm around her and offered her a bite of grilled cheese. She declined with a polite smile. It was nice to see they were still together and had moved forward after all that they had gone through with that awful flighter crash. I looked at G.W. and how pristine he looked and thought it really was unbelievable that he had bounced right back to normal after that.

"Right, babe? We love Doro, don't we?!"

"Of course! Actually, Doro, can I steal you for a minute for a bathroom break?"

"Let's go." I stuffed the last bite of grilled cheese into my mouth. "Real butter, so good!"

G.W. laughed as we walked away.

Brittany and I made our way through the super chatty crowd and down the hall. I noticed an excess of men in black posted up all over the place, in front of every doorway.

We went into the bathroom. We entered separate stalls and

peed then came out to wash our hands. There was another lady in there who smiled at us. I was about to head out, but Brittany held me back and waited for the lady to leave before pulling me into a stall and shutting the door behind us.

Brittany flushed the toilet and spoke with her words hushed under the sound of the flush. "I've wanted to talk to you but I couldn't until we were somewhere private."

"What's up? Is everything okay?"

"Yes. I want to hear about your trip."

I wanted to tell her about my trip, and what a trip it was, but I was limited in more ways than one. We had been really open with each other the last couple of times we hung out, and it threw me off that I had to keep quiet now. It was like nobody could know the complete story with me, myself included, and that kind of hit me in the gut.

"We can discuss that later though, because we don't have much time," she said.

I was off the hook for now. She went on, "Doro, you need to watch out for yourself and be very discerning with what you're being told right now."

"I know. I'm always watching out."

"I know you are. But I also know all this departing mission stuff can sound really attractive. The underlying truth to it is very scary."

"I know it's scary to think the Earth is almost to the point of being uninhabitable. But it is pretty incredible that they've come so far with a solution for a fresh start like this, isn't it?"

"In some ways, yes, but in other ways it's completely terrible to be honest."

I had to play devil's advocate in order to keep the information coming from each and every perspective on my path.

"In what ways?"

"It is all about those in power usurping complete power."

"That's what I was thinking in Seneca, that it was exclusive and what about everyone else in the Aboves? But isn't this different? Isn't this an opportunity for everyone to start fresh and have a good life— on Mars."

Brittany flushed the toilet in our small bathroom stall again and spoke super low and close to me. "Right now these people control the atmosphere on Earth and are systematically making it bad enough that they can convince people to leave Earth to want to live on Mars. They have a way to create an atmosphere on Mars and they are setting up to do it right now, as we speak. They have already recruited millions of people to commit to setting up a colony there so that they can then mine and control all the resources, and the people that come there, too. They have the capability to repair the atmosphere here but they are *choosing* not to because, if they did, people would choose to stay here. Then there wouldn't be anyone to do all their dirty work while keeping them rich and in power."

The sound of the flushing stopped and was replaced by the sound of the door to the bathroom opening. We went dead silent inside our stall. Outside of it we heard a voice—

"Dorothy?" It was Jennifer Wallingsford.

Brittany threw her finger up to her lip to say, "Shhh."

"No, it's Brittany," Brittany replied.

"Oh. G.W. said Doro went to the bathroom."

"Yes, I saw her washing her hands on my way in."

"Okay."

Jennifer didn't sound too sold. I hoped she wouldn't look under the door to the stall. I didn't want to get caught in this super awkward lie. Something was going on between these two and I definitely didn't want to get embroiled in it.

"If you do see her, please let her know my flighter is ready to go back," Jennifer said.

"Sure, no problem," Brittany replied.

Jennifer left the bathroom.

"I want to tell you more but I can't here," Brittany said. "We'll talk when we get back to Seneca. Wait a few and then come out," Brittany whispered to me.

Brittany stepped out and I was left alone to take a deep breath and collect my thoughts. I really needed to get back so I could dig deeper into the memories I was missing. They'd let me better decipher everything that was going on because I'd be more *me* than the person I was masquerading as now.

38

ON THE BRINK of rush hour, Jennifer and I took our flighter ride back to the ascension dome. I noticed many more flighters in the air than the last time I was in Washington, D.C. Jennifer appeared to be a bit pensive as she looked out the window.

"Is everything okay?" I asked.

"Yes. I just miss my parents. My dad's been so busy lately with the Mars mission, and my mom with her foundation, that my family hasn't spent a lot of time together."

"I can relate to that."

"I know you can. I know it's all worth it, though, and soon we will all be in a position to be together, forever, in a whole new world."

"Literally," I added with a little laugh. It was funny because it sounded too good to be true, and no matter how cool it would be for inhabiting another planet to become a reality, I wouldn't believe it until I was standing on red soil looking back at the Pale Blue Dot from millions of miles away.

I was alerted that I had an incoming flex from Ellen and I kind of froze up. I didn't want to squash this solid rapport between Jennifer and myself by jumping into a conversation with Ellen, so I shot her a flex message.

Hey, Ellen, I'm with a friend, I'll flex you back later.

Sounds good. Talk soon.

I would connect with Ellen when I was back in the youth residences on my own.

"Listen," Jennifer said. "I don't ever want to talk behind anyone's back, and I think Brittany is a really sweet person. My brother clearly adores her. But the rest of her family doesn't have our best interest in mind, politically speaking."

My flex notification went off again. This time it was my mom.

I hit 'accept' in my mind and my mom came through.

Honey, how is your head? Are you home from session now?

Hi, Mom! I'm okay. I'm out with my friend, Jennifer Wallingsford. Home soon. Don't worry about me. I promise I will be in bed soon and will connect with you later.

Okay. Can I bring you a bite?

Maybe tomorrow. I just had a grilled cheese.

Okay, honey. I love you.

Love you, Mom.

I tried to do all that flexing quickly so Jennifer wouldn't notice I was doing it at all— from my implant, but I think I just came across as aloof.

"Everything okay?" Jennifer asked.

"Yes, completely, I was just thinking I forgot to flex my mom and she's probably worried."

"Soon you can let her know just how okay you are. Better than okay. I am literally dreaming of the sunsets from a new perspective with the people I love. These dreams are something I won't ever let anyone take away from me."

"Of course you shouldn't"

"Right? Sadly, if it was up to some people, we'd all die suffering in an apocalyptic wasteland just on the existential principal that Earth is our home."

"Home is where the heart is," I said.

On the acoustic carrier ride back into the youth residences a B3 Media broadcast played overhead on monitors. News anchor Becky Hudson reported over video images of a towering cylindrical structure filled with bubbling blue liquid.

"Seneca's brainchild, The Doromium Project, that has been underway on the Martian planet for three years now is coming back with initial tests showing the blockage of Carbon Dioxide from entering the atmosphere. If everything goes according to plan, people will be walking on the red planet without any special space gear in a matter of a couple of years."

Video images of humans in spacesuits walking on Mars and waving to the camera intercut with a Senecan flag waving in the breeze.

"And in less than ten years, the Mars we will know will no longer be red but instead covered by emerald green rolling hills and the first generation of Senecan settlers. These are projections of what we expect to see in under a decade."

Video images show renderings of: Green forests with red mountains in the background. Manmade lakes being filled with rain pouring from clouds, humans walking on a planet, children playing, the first Martians— the next generation of human evolution.

Everyone on the acoustic carrier watched in amazement and shared in a moment of excitement that really seemed to instill in all of us a sense of camaraderie. We looked around, smiling at one another with big hopeful eyes, but underneath my projected enthusiasm I felt a growing awareness of the media's manipulation.

39

IT WAS LATER than I expected by the time I got back to my room in the residences, and the day's excitement had me worn down. I knew I should go to sleep, but I had to put sleep on the backburner. I needed to get through a large enough chunk of memories in order to feel I'd been productive.

When I walked into the bathroom, I caught a reflection of myself in the mirror and was shocked by the horrendous dark bags under my eyes. I took a quick shower and used my mouth brush. After I was in my pajamas, I drank a cup of water as I sat on the edge of my bed, gearing up for a journey into the archives of my memories. I was just too tired to sit up in a chair at my desk. I had gotten used to the lingering headache that so far was more a nuisance then a debilitation. I just hoped it wouldn't worsen and that the water would help me maintain. I so could have used a mocha, but I wasn't about to put myself in the same position I had last time, curled up in the fetal position for two days or more.

I pulled up my Veil and entered my memory database at the point where I had left off last time. There was a really strong memory that took up a lot of space by copying itself in multiple locations in my brain, so I dove right into it. I was instantly enthralled with meeting one of the most intriguing people I think I've ever come across in my entire life. His gripping green eyes stormed into my mind like thunder and lightning. This guy in his Jimmy Cliff shirt was fierce yet peaceful. He nursed me back to health and he told me his name was Jadel.

There was no question in my mind that this was a sequence of memories I needed to keep. Who was Jadel and what had become of him and our relationship before I made it back here to the NeuroQuE procedure? I realized that, although I had been productive so far in my memory dig, I would not get to sleep until I got to the bottom of this Jadel storyline. It would behoove me to reinsert every memory from my experience with Jadel because, if I had inserted fragmented memories of my time with him, it might mess up my recollection process down the line.

I revisited the oddest experience. This beautiful guy, Jadel, offered me a river snail to eat. The sensory experience replayed inside of me as if I was there: the shriveled, rubbery texture against my tongue mixed with the smell of dank post-storm air that was a stew of humid earth and boiling snail meat. I was suddenly so nauseous that I had to run to my toilet and throw up.

I knew that memory was one I needed to replant, but as I

crouched over the toilet, I just wanted it to vanish, so I let it slip away.

I started to become confused. Why was I over my toilet? Should I move forward away from whatever memory had me vomiting or should I go backwards because it might be something I would need in the future? I didn't want to replay the memory because it might make me get sick again. I decided that I couldn't handle any more physical burden while my mind was in the midst of such an exhausting workout, so I made a judgement call to move forward.

This process was not something for the faint of heart. I was so spent from vomiting that I couldn't walk back to my bed from the toilet. I had to crawl. My head was so heavy that I needed to lie down. I made it to the edge of my bed, reached up, gripped my covers on top of my mattress and pulled myself up onto my bed. I hit the mattress with a thunk. I let myself focus on my breath until I was fully present in it.

Then I hit the archives of my mind again and dug deeper and deeper, replanting memory after memory after memory. Entering Hub 48, being chased by S.O.I.L., finding out Jadel was on the inside, questioning his motive, hiding from Jadel, being recaptured by a group that ended up being my friends in disguise. Anika had come with Reba, Dom, and a new guy from inside the hub, Giancarlo. But the memory that broke my flow and threw me back into my waking conscious state was when

Dom gave me this beautiful moonstone necklace I was wearing. I held it softly between my fingers and wanted to linger there in that memory, and so I did until I drifted off.

40

WITH A FEW blinks I narrowly escaped the clutches of a bizarre dream. My feet had been stuck in muddy quicksand and I was calling out for help. Thick storm clouds were approaching with deep growls of thunder that suppressed the sound of my cries. Nobody would have heard me, so even though I woke with a cloudy head and a hollow stomach, I was glad to have been liberated from that nightmare.

I was face down, curled into a mound of clamminess on my bed. I'd taken all my pajamas off. My damp tank top and underwear clung to my skin. I was cold and numb in my limbs. I reached for my pajama top but it was drenched with sweat so I hopped up to grab a dry sweatshirt. Dizziness engulfed me. My head flopped to the side like a bag of marbles. The space between my ears started to shrink and expand, and my eyes were being squeezed out of their sockets. I grabbed at my ears to try and hold it all in.

A crevice formed between my eyelids and I caught a glimpse

of the time— two o'clock! I'd blown straight through the night and into the next day as if time didn't exist.

I needed to flex Dom. I was at the tippy-top of my awareness that Dom and I had made it past the issues we had when I left for South America. Amidst all this brain bashing I yearned for just a sliver of affection to help push me along.

My flexer went nuts and I couldn't pull up my contacts. Not a single one. I could barely see because the pounding in my head was too strong, like cymbals being smashed together over and over again, louder and louder, causing my eyes to pop out of their sockets. Electric shocks fired off down through my lungs and into my toes. My toes curled up and my legs cramped. I couldn't make it stop!

I wailed in pain.

My flexer alerts started going haywire.

It was Ellen:

Doro stay put, I'm on my way.

Then Reba:

Don't worry, Doro, I will be right there!

Suddenly, a doctor— the one from Claytor Lake, Dr. Cairncross, beamed through in FigureFlex;

Miss Campbell, I need you to come back to my center at Claytor Lake immediately.

Then Dom popped through:

Doro, I got a flex from you, but it keeps saying you're off the grid. Meet me at Ty's after session.

Dr. Cairncross again:

This is extremely urgent. You are having dangerous brain activity. I advise you to drop whatever you are doing, find Ellen Malone, and come right away.

Ring, ring, ring at my door.

I pulled as much air into my lungs as possible, pushed myself up to a seated position and screamed in pain from the cramp that rippled through my right calf muscle. I couldn't move a single centimeter.

Through gritted teeth I flex commanded my door to open. It was Reba. He darted in. I then ordered the door to shut behind him.

"Reba—"

"Campbella, I knew something was up."

The cramp subsided quickly and I was relieved on multiple levels, but indescribably weak. "Thank god you're here. You're such a good friend. I haven't been a good friend to you."

"Forget *me*. You haven't been a good friend to *yourself*."

"Please help me."

"I'm getting a doctor."

"No! Please… I don't want a doctor." I panted and rubbed at my head near my temples, trying to release a vice grip of stress.

"Well, what do you want to do? Flex your mom?"

"No! Not my mom, she will freak out."

"You're freaking *me* out. Your eyes are spinning into the back of your head! You could have a seizure or a heart attack! We need help. I can't help you. We need someone."

"Ahhh! Just... just..." I knew something wasn't right, but Reba didn't know the NeuroQuE doctor and I didn't want my mom to see me like this. "I just need Ellen to get here already."

"Why Ellen?" Reba asked.

"She's the only one who knows where I need to go."

I could see Reba's wheels turning as his eyes shifted from side to side. He calmly said, "I feel she's a part of of the reason that got you into this state."

In a way he was right. But so was I.

"She's not. This is all me. Ahhh!" I tucked my head down under my pillow and screamed out in pain.

"Oh, Doro, your pain is killing me," Reba gripped his hand on my shoulder. I could feel we were one in the same for a moment. Ever the empath, he was inhaling my agony. I had to find a way to make the pain stop.

My doorbell rang again.

"I'll protect you," Reba assured me. But I could tell that, even though he wanted to protect me, he didn't think he had that capability against what or who was out there beyond the door.

Ellen and Dom announced themselves.

I flex commanded my door to open.

Ellen and Dom rushed in. Dom crouched down on the floor in

front of me and took my hands, "I've been looking everywhere for you. I went to S.E.R.C., The Cantina, Ty's, and came by three times!"

"I'm sorry, Dom."

"Don't apologize and don't worry about anything right now. All we need to do is make sure you're okay."

Ellen wasn't her calm self in the least bit. "I knew something was wrong when you never flexed me back."

"She needs a doctor," Reba asserted.

I could sense Dom wanted to take charge here and take care of me. I appreciated that so much. Clearly I messed up big time. I needed help.

Ellen sat down next to Dom and spoke to me, very gently by Ellen standards, "Doro, we're going to take you back to Claytor Lake." She leaned in as to only whisper this to me, "I got the call from Dr. Cairncross. You need to get in there immediately."

Reba nervously rubbed at his head, saying, "Whoa!" and stepped up to Ellen. "Right now she needs a doctor to come see her right here, and not to go to any secret place where they keep doing crazy procedures on her."

"We appreciate your concern, Timothy, but this issue Doro has is beyond traditional medicine."

"Okay, I don't know exactly what is going on but I do know she is worse than the last time I saw her, before you took her to Clayton Lake. I know that's where you took her. She didn't have to tell me."

Ellen shot him a look. "You're out of line, and if you don't mind your business, you're not only going to make this worse for Doro, but for yourself, too."

"Please stop," I muttered.

"See!" Reba spat. "She's in pain!"

Dom caressed my back, "I'm staying with you this time, no matter what."

I gently smiled at him.

"Can you get up, Doro?" Dom asked.

I shook my head.

"I'll carry her," Dom said to Ellen.

Reba moved directly in front of them. "Don't do this, you guys."

Dom moved face-to-face with Reba, "You need to back off, buddy. Just go home."

Ellen held my hand. "You're freezing," she said. "Let's get you into some comfortable clothes."

Reba stood firm. "Stop pushing her into some fight that is not worth her life! Look at her. It's killing her!"

"Don't let them brainwash you, too," Dom snapped at Reba.

"I can't be brainwashed!" He retorted.

"Everybody can be brainwashed," Dom replied.

Ellen helped me get my sweatshirt on. Reba wasn't having it. "I just know that swimming upstream in the river never got anyone anywhere. We have to go with the flow and stay above water. Ellen is making Doro do the opposite of that and it needs to stop before she drowns!"

"The fact that you just said that proves they've got you, too," Dom asserted.

"And what about you, Ellen?" Reba forcefully asked. I'd never seen him so pushy before.

"Sure, me too. At one point, I was. But I have been digesting information since you were in diapers, Timothy, and I can tell you precisely what's going on right now."

"I don't need to be told to understand."

"Actually, yes, you do. Sometimes information is more valuable than what you *feel* or to whom you sense your allegiance. Doro's unique situation is that she has a flex implant. Therefore, she is forever vulnerable, whereas her father does not have the implant. Her implant was hacked by Flexer Technology because they didn't want her getting to her dad. They believed if she had, she would have found information that the Departers could use to their advantage. There is a technological battle for mind control of Doro between multiple factions."

"*You* are in one of those factions!" Reba shouted.

"And you?" Ellen calmly queried of him.

"The Intuerians have an allegiance to the people that made us a part of a society that cherishes us, unlike the Aboves where we were treated like monsters. We just want to be a part of a good life like every other human being. And they are making that dream a reality."

"So, the Departers are using mind-control and brainwashing on Doro because she is the only one who can get close enough to influence her dad, and she's the only one with a mathematical acumen on par with his… and you can get behind that because of your *allegiance*?" Ellen asked him.

I was completely thrown in that moment but too sick to react. I could barely move or see at this point.

Reba sat down next to me and his voice quieted a bit. "I wasn't aware."

Ellen replied, "We know you weren't. And we know you have no ill intent."

"I don't," Reba assured me, "I just don't want you to feel like this."

Dom's patience for the back and forth was shot. "I don't care about anything but seeing to it that Doro is given the chance to make her own decisions and *nobody* is taking advantage of her."

I had to make a choice. It was weird because, going into this moment, I was standing strong, arm-linked with my friend, Reba, who seemed to be connected to me more so than anyone else. Then I started playing through every fact, and everything presented by Ellen, and I was overloaded with information. It was all contradictory and made my head spin. I couldn't see a straight line to what was right.

"Doro?" Dom looked pleadingly at me, and the second I caught his gaze none of that mattered. Every hand I'd ever played, every dollar I'd ever made, the flighters I'd jacked, the mainframe I'd hacked, factions, Aboves, Earth, Mars… none of it mattered. There was only one truth here that I knew and it came from within.

I looked at each one of them. "Let's go."

41

THE TRIP FROM my residence to C-QNCE was a bit of a blur. I know I was spoken to, and I spoke back, but nothing stuck. This was a literal experience of 'in one ear and out the other.' It was as if my brain could no longer accept memories in their complete form because I had been so immersed in re-implanting the old ones. I didn't know old from new. I just kept hearing Ellen say, "We are going to reboot you."

I nodded. My forehead contorted as did the muscles in my entire body. I struggled to hang on to any thought I could wrap my head around, but I just couldn't. Each one came and went, slipping away as a mass of blankness expanded in my mind.

My one stipulation in coming here had been that I would only leave my residence if Dom was by my side the entire time. He was my one and only partner in crime. My solid rock in the raging river. I should have known that from the moment we'd shared in the water at Difficult Run, around the time when we first met, and I should have held on to him and never let him go.

I wouldn't make that mistake again.

I couldn't even see straight enough to make out what, or who, was two feet in front of me. I got flashes of light and dark, and bits and pieces of dialogue from Dr. Cairncross, Ellen and Dom. My stomach crackled and constricted like it was eating itself. My throat burned. My hand gripped Dom's, but my strength slowly slipped away along with my mind and there was nothing I could do to hang on.

Time seemed to move in snippets, and the next thing I knew, I was being submerged back into the NeuroQuE's saline tank.

The white flashing lights began streaming to infinity and beyond. I was scared to death as my body started to convulse. That didn't happen last time. Something felt terribly unfamiliar and awry. I flailed my arms hoping they would get me out. I didn't care about my memories anymore. The machines could have them. I just wanted to live. I lost control of my body. Everything felt wrong. Terror rippled from me into the saline.

But then my fear was smothered into a disappearing heap as I was vacuumed up into a dome of warm, creamy light above the saline. I took one massive breath of sacred air and I never breathed it back out.

As my soul was warmed by the light, everything suddenly made sense: Love. With every piece of my heart, love. Drench the world in it as I was being drenched in it now. With every single solitary ounce of love that I pour out, shower my own self generously in it, too. I had been too hard on everyone. I was too hard on myself. I had been so absorbed by the shots firing off inside my skull that I wasn't trusting in the limitless potential of my soul.

I practically suffocated myself to death with questions of trust on the outside while all along the answer was inside me. All this twisting and turning through the spaces that I could see with my own two eyes, agonizing over what was true and what was false, overthinking other people's motives and the pragmatism of my own agenda, I had zoomed right past the most important part of it all. Love.

There was a shushing sound as I moved into a funnel of light and everything became incredibly bright. Nothing but light. There was no more pain. No more headaches. No more confusion.

With total weightlessness I rose above the NeuroQuE and I looked down from about ten feet up. The first thing I saw was my lifeless body on a medical table, being tended to by several doctors and nurses and machines. I wasn't worried. I was fine. That body wasn't me. This consciousness was me and here I was.

I saw Dom. He was losing it, right next to my body, begging, pleading, caressing my face, shaking my hand, gripping my arm. All I could hear were muffled voices. They were filled with panic and despair, and I just wanted to let them know it would be okay. They tried to revive me with every tool they had, but nothing would work. That was there and I was here.

I was present. I was exactly where I needed to be. Finally. The chaos behind and before me was an illusion. I was enveloped in a warm hug as I watched the mania of thoughts and emotions transpire. There was no more pain. There were no more worries. I wanted to shed some of this peace for all of the people down there.

Dom had his cheek pressed to mine. Tears streamed down his face. He was clenching his jaw and shaking his head. He was hysterical. Ellen tried to pull him away at the nurse's command.

Swirling clouds of gray smoke seeped into the room and I didn't want them to suffocate Dom. I didn't want them to touch any of the people that surrounded my body, trying to resuscitate it. The good in their hearts was abundant and beautiful. It made the love inside me swell.

That gray smoke was a slow creeping evil, and I felt, if I could drift up higher and reach the peaceful light above, I could bring it back down to extinguish the madness. As the dim blizzard of warmth engulfed my vision, the last thing that I glimpsed was the monitor of my stats below— my pulse flatlined. That beating mass of muscle in my chest stopped and all that was any longer was stillness.

As I blissfully floated in an infinite sea of peace, these two astonishingly powerful little balls of illumination sailed in my direction and circulated around me, and then I connected with one—

Reba.

Hello again.

Where are we?

Follow me.

Rayya Deeb is a mother, wife, writer and Virginia Tech Hokie, born in London, England and raised in Northern Virginia. Seneca Element is her sophomore novel. She lives in Southern California with her husband and two daughters. Visit her at www.rayyadeeb.com

Printed in Dunstable, United Kingdom